Grace Of The Clouds

by
Michelina Pagano

PublishAmerica

Baltimore

First printing

ISBN: 1-59129-764-8
PUBLISHED BY PUBLISHAMERICA BOOK
PUBLISHERS
www.publishamerica.com
Baltimore

Printed in the United States of America

For my grandmothers
Olimpia and Michela,
who taught me the wisdom of life.

And to all those dearly departed,
may we find their spirits in the passing clouds watching over us.

4/03
Dear Anita
May the Cloud work
magic in your life!
All my love

To my sweet husband Tony, my who taught me the meaning of love.

I wish to express my appreciation to my parents, Mary and Dom, my sister and brother Olimpia and Frank for believing in me and to my entire family whose colorful tales and spirited lives inspired me to write. I would like to thank the countless friends and relatives who've patiently read each rewrite with support and encouragement. In particular, I'd like to thank Estelle, for her referral. I'd especially like to thank Michele, Gina, Janis, Marie, Rodd, Fran, Maddie and Sam for their work in helping to refine and promote this book. And, to my Navajo friends Lena, Jones, Jaron and Lynnette, who welcomed me with great hospitality into the Navajo Nation and taught me the beauty of Native American culture.

Sometimes gentle, sometimes capricious, sometimes awful,
never the same for two moments together;
almost human in its passions, almost spiritual in its tenderness,
almost Divine in its infinity.

~ John Ruskin
"The Sky"

CHAPTER ONE

This is a story about a mysterious butte that once stood on the western horizon of Arizona near the mystical town of Sedona. Like the many red rocks of the Southwestern canyons, this one had a name too. The locals called it Finger's Edge. This was no ordinary rock. They say the tall, thin butte was Earth's finger reaching from the dirt to touch the belly of Heaven. The Navajos say the place it once stood is now considered sacred land. Visitors claim it's the place that spawned a hundred love stories. Yet, it is the little known legend about Grace of the Clouds and her peculiar love story that still echoes through the canyons.

~

It happened sometime in the late 1800's, when there was still unrest between the Native Americans and the pioneers, when parts of the Southwest were still governed by Mexico. During this time, the local Indians believed a legend that told of a day when a Great One, born of dirt and clouds, would unite all people, living and dead. This story trickled down through generations of Native Americans living among the red rocks who waited hundreds of years for the big event. They didn't know exactly when it would happen, but they knew where – at junction of land and sky, on the sacred butte they called Finger's Edge.

Dancing Wind waited all her life for this grand moment, the one she was born for. Her life's purpose was reflected in her name, which meant, *one who danced between Heaven and Earth,* and was thus destined to foster the offspring of the divine. Dancing Wind, losing time and patience, weathered nearly three-quarters of a century in anxious anticipation for a Great One who never came.

The desert land swallowed her up and pickled her like a prune. Coal eyes stared out from her leather face. Elmo rescued her from the claws of vicious white men who destroyed her clan, her family, her home and her life. The kind and gentle stranger recognized the injustice and hardship the Navajos suffered. When he found Dancing Wind near death, he welcomed her to his home and gave her life again. In return, she promised to soothe his land and mind his beasts, making her home on the huge ranch Elmo Zander owned. She didn't mind. To Dancing Wind, it was the forceful hand of fate that put her at the foot of Finger's Edge.

As she caressed the land and nurtured the creatures, she couldn't help but gaze wistfully at the majestic profile of Finger's Edge. It was a daily reminder of her destiny. Aware of the brittleness of her bones, the rustiness of her flesh, she knew she didn't have much time left above the soil. This was one of the things that troubled her soul daily.

The other was Matilda.

~

No one knew why Elmo ever married the big and hairy Matilda, or even named his ranch after her. Some speculated she entertained him with her stubborn temper and charmed him with her broad physique, a woman standing well over six feet with shoulders that spanned the width of a doorway. She was blessed with one magnificent eyebrow, which adorned her forehead like black fur. Her mustache had to be combed daily to retain its fine, silky texture and her chin was knobbed with long, stringy wires. Matilda captured his heart.

Elmo met her on a business trip in Las Placitas, the bartender in a loud and rowdy saloon called Casa Grande. Matilda amused the wealthy American rancher with her fast shooting and shot drinking. Her clever banter and witty remarks somehow found a way deep into Elmo's heart. He felt great compassion for her and recognized something special in her spirit. Matilda was like no woman he ever met. She was a one of a kind. Elmo snatched a rare breed, a diamond still in the dirt. He saw something in her that no one was able to see, even if they stretched their imaginations until it fell out of their heads. Someplace, buried beneath her robust flesh, he saw her beauty.

That day, Elmo took her home with him to the new ranch he named in her honor, "Big Matilda," which later became "Big M."

Although Elmo was blind to her temper, the rest of the ranch wasn't. To them, Matilda was an intolerable mistress who demanded the impossible. She hated all the help on Big M, with the exception of Amando Lopez. Besides being a fellow Mexican, he was the only one who indulged her crazy tales of witches.

Matilda believed she was cursed. She experienced misfortune all her life and everywhere she went she found bad luck. The oldest of twelve and the last to marry, her mother told her she was born without a guardian angel as a the result of a witch's spell cast upon the Arroyo family. The hex, she was told, affected the first born of their family and whomever they married. The affliction made her ugly, unlucky and bitter. Until it was broken, this curse promised to doom her first born as well as the first born of generations to follow.

All of Mexico knew this and every man avoided her, which wasn't very hard to do. Aside from her stupendous appearance, her fury sent big men screaming for their mothers. Matilda was quite a package, which was why Elmo's initial attempts at wooing were met with such suspicion. It was an experience Matilda never felt before, one that silenced her roar for a while. When he married her, Matilda thought her luck finally changed.

But shortly after Matilda gave birth to Ben, Elmo mysteriously disappeared. Matilda was left alone with a bitter rage, a small child and a big ranch.

Elmo Zander was never seen again.

~

Ben tried not to upset his mother. He walked quietly around her, careful not to make too much noise. Despite Matilda's strict orders to stay away from "Dirty Wind," Ben managed to sneak away in the afternoons when he knew Matilda was busy expending her wrath on any quivering ranch hand who happened to be in her way.

Dancing Wind was Ben's one and only friend, his escape from the routine chaos of a failing ranch and a bitter mother. She lived in a small, round *Hogan* made from log and earth, filled with things to look at. Dancing Wind's home was decorated with Navajo art, things she made and collected.

Four clay jars marked the east, south, west and north walls of her home. Dancing Wind told Ben that each jar contained an element of life. The East jar contained the flesh of Earth. The South jar preserved tears from the clouds. The West jar captured the smoke of fire and the North jar held the wind's breath. A tear-shaped net made of cowhide, wood and feathers hung above her bed to catch bad dreams. All these things were there to protect her and give her strength for the task she was destined to do.

The East wall bore a large, worn bead tapestry that illustrated Finger's Edge touching a puffy cloud. Dancing Wind pointed to it.

"There is sacred ground at the top of Finger's Edge. It is forbidden to walk there."

A flickering flame ignited every crevasse of Dancing Wind's face as she began her story. Charcoal eyes glistened from her leather skin. Ben looked at the old woman and his eyes grew wide with intrigue.

"It's where Mother Earth and Father Sky come together. And, one day a Great One will be born from their union. And that's when my task will finally begin."

Ben listened closely, fascinated by the gravel texture of her voice, which vibrated throughout his body. The campfire in the center of the circular room sent smoke streaming through a small opening in the ceiling. The crackle of wood snapped in the quiet gap. She began again, softly.

"This Child made from dirt and cloud will bring great love to all of us, both living and dead."

Dancing Wind blinked and looked at the eager child whose eyes grew dark with curiosity.

"Will there be ghosts?"

Dancing Wind smiled at the little boy and shook her head. "The living and the dead are made from the same Spirit. We are all ghosts."

"Is the Great One a ghost, too?"

"The Great One is the Great Spirit."

"Is he God?"

"He is the God in all of us," Dancing Wind smiled at the boy's earnest attempt to understand something beyond his years. At five years old, the wheels of Ben's brain whirled in search for a truth. He needed to know the facts in order to choose between Dancing Wind's story and his mother's.

Dancing Wind and Ben sat on sheepskin rugs that protected them from the cold, dirt floor of the Hogan.

"The Great One will come in peace. He will be a great warrior who will have the wisdom of the land and the power of the heavens. He will know all and speak without words because the wind will be his voice. The sky will be his eye so he can look at the Earth and see it all at once."

Dancing Wind's gaze fell upon the single window on the west wall of her home and saw the rock looming in the distance. The remaining light from the fading day caused her eyes to grow darker.

"When?" Ben's brows were in a knot. "When is he coming?"

"When the wind sings and clouds cry feathers." Her eyes drifted in the twilight sky.

"Dancing Wind?"

She broke her trance to look at the boy. Ben looked in each of her eyes, seeking an answer to a question he did not ask. Her smile sent a thousand wrinkles across her cheeks. Once he tried to count the lines that mapped her flesh but ran out of numbers. To Ben, she held the wisdom of decades and the answers to life. Dancing Wind took a soft breath and read the boy's eyes. She answered quietly.

"Don't worry, Ben. One day your father will return to you."

The hesitation on the small face broke with a faint smile.

"But where is he?"

Dancing Wind had a way of calming his fears.

"He is around, little one."

"Where?"

"In the air, in the walls of your home, in your heart."

"But why did he leave?" Ben could not understand. His eyes pleaded with Dancing Wind. "Did you see him when he left us?"

"No, Ben, I did not see him. I don't know where he went or why he left, but once I dreamed of a gentle white man who left his family to do a great deed." She gently brushed the brown hair from Ben's eyes.

"And when he is done, he will come back with peace in his heart to share with you and your mother."

Her voice was like a goose feather blanket that made him feel warm and protected. She gathered him into her arms and rubbed his head. Ben's large, brown eyes looked up at hers, puzzled.

"My mother will have peace, too?"

Dancing Wind nodded as she slowly rocked the boy. "Yes, little one, your mother will have peace, too, one day."

Ben snuggled in Dancing Wind's arms, feeling the warmth of her round body. Ben couldn't understand why his mother didn't like her.

"Then maybe," he began in a whisper, "she won't be so bad to you anymore."

Dancing Wind looked at the fire.

"One day your mother will understand that our God is the same God."

~

The red rock on the horizon gleamed in the pink light of dawn. Ben watched how Dancing Wind gazed at Finger's Edge. Every morning she rose early to greet it with a prayer. With her eyes closed, she stretched her ancient hands toward it, as if trying to extract life. She prayed to Finger's Edge, to the sun and to the wind in a chant that rang with Navajo rhythm.

"Everyone," she once told him, "has a song. A song tells the world who we are."

Ben wished he could see what she saw in the mysterious butte she stared at so lovingly. It was quite different from how his mother looked at it.

"That evil rock!" she called it.

Matilda never spoke, she always yelled.

"You stay away from that place!" she warned him. "It's where the witches live!"

Matilda ordered him never, ever to go near Finger's Edge. She believed it was where sorceresses schooled themselves in devil worship. She filled Ben with horror stories of incantations she witnessed. Once, while riding to Las Placitas, she saw a woman scream some words, and off she went, gliding into the sky, flying like a Raven. *That* was a witch. She constantly warned Ben to be careful. Finger's Edge was part of their curse and must be avoided at all costs. She forbade Ben to even look upon the wickedest butte of the West.

Amando told her about Finger's Edge when she first came to the ranch. He used to see a strange cloud of green smoke occasionally spewing from its tip. It was a brew, he insisted, a rancid recipe made from dead goats and human heads.

"I tell you, before Elmo came, there was a man who went up there," he said as he unraveled a tale in a thick Spanish accent. "A man with skin and bones just like you and me."

Amando Lopez liked to smoke when he told stories. The smoke trailed up and collided with the wide rim of his worn sombrero, where it left an ominous stain. His tales made Matilda swoon and gave Ben nightmares.

"And do you know what happened?"

His pauses were always longer than necessary. His black eyes sparkled. "He disappeared...."

That's precisely when Matilda's nostrils expanded to suck all the air in the thick silence.

"BUT!"

Amando liked to startle the room with his sudden bursts.

"Do you know, they found his body weeks later *without any bones?*"

Amando nodded, proud of his stories. He knew them all.

Matilda always listened closely to Amando's fables. He was the only one on all of Big M who earned her ear and respect, a confidant in the passing years without Elmo. Amando took another drag from his cigarette and let the smoke fall from his lips in a stream his hat routinely intercepted.

"No worry, Señora. My son Juan will protect us from all the

brujas." He stood up from his chair. "You know, I named him for such a purpose."

"I know! I know!" Matilda rolled her eyes with a huff.

She knew as well as Amando that according to Mexican superstition, persons named Juan had special power over witches and were able to repel them.

Amando relished another puff before allowing circles of smoke emerge from his lips.

"But Señora, if you are very concerned over these witches, I can give you a recipe to protect you."

Matilda bolted up from her chair.

"Amando! I want that recipe!" she shouted.

Amando found humor in her extreme emotions.

"Señora, I suggest you find ink and paper to write this down," he gestured with his cigarette. Matilda's brow fell heavy on her eyes.

"You foolish Mexican, do you think I am so stupid that I can not remember a simple spell?"

Amando sighed and surrendered to her whim with a shrug.

He gave Matilda the most powerful spell he knew of and instructed her to use the recipe only when she felt the certain presence of bad luck and evil spirits.

Combine in one small wooden bowl, these items:
1 lock of hair
1 puff of breath
1 tear
1 pinch of salt
1 handful of soil
Once the ingredients are together, hold the bowl above one's head and chant these words three times:
"With the force of good, my spirit will repel the bad away from me and evil will fall away from the earth and away from my soul."

"Are you sure you do not want to write this down?" Amando asked as he watched Matilda mouth the words to herself, repeating after him. Stubbornly, she insisted on committing the spell to memory, forcing Amando to recite the recipe over and over. It was a new formula, one that she would surely use in case of emergency.

"Señora, this spell is very powerful. It must be used sparingly. I recommend using it only once. For all other fears, I must prescribe another potion."

Matilda nodded and sat down again, transfixed by the words of the spell that rattled in her head. Amando watched her curiously and bit on his cigarette. He was amused.

"Señora, I have much work to do."

The hinged door smacked shut as Amando left the house. Matilda gazed at the door long after he was gone. She knew that as long as they stayed away from Finger's Edge they would, in some way, be safe. It was ill fate that placed her directly in the valley of the witches.

Matilda practiced other rituals besides those taught to her by Amando. As an extra safeguard, she forced the ranch hands to put cornhusk crosses on the ears of all the stock. She also fashioned a cross from two broom straws and placed it in the door frame to prevented any witch from entering her home. Matilda did everything to protect herself from the evil that lurked on the fringes of Big M. But her methods were in vain.

CHAPTER TWO

Night fell upon Big M like a velvet cloak that smothered it from sight. This night, however, was darker than most and its dense silence was only broken by the cries of crickets.

After bustling about the house, finishing up the last of the paperwork she so much dreaded, Matilda fell into her favorite armchair. She gulped down a steaming cup of tea as she sank into the groaning red leather, whose arms ached from accommodating Matilda's broad backside. Something caught her eye.

She noticed a strange movement out the window. Perhaps a nearby tree created the fleeting shadow in the clouded moonlight, but to Matilda, it looked suspicious. She grabbed a rifle and like a hunter, posed discretely by the open window, slipped the barrel into the cool air and aimed at the thick black night.

A shot rang out. The bullet ricocheted off a tree and awakened some ranch hands. At that moment, Matilda thought she saw the electrifying silhouette of a witch. She shut the window with a slam and flew into the kitchen.

Inside the large oak wood cupboard, she scrambled for a bowl but not just any bowl, even though she owned many, from fine china to finely painted ceramic. She sought a simple wooden one and found it.

Matilda chopped a lock of her thick, black hair into the bowl. Then she blinked several times and squeezed her eyes tightly, as she tried to extract the next ingredient the potion called for. She reached for a rotting onion and sliced it. She waved its pungent fumes over her eyes but still no tears appeared. In frustration, she sighed, cleared her throat and instead, spit into the bowl, assuming it was a good substitute for a tear. She sprinkled a pinch of salt on the mixture and breathed one long, hot puff of soggy breath on top of it all. Matilda reached out the open kitchen window, dug her gamy hand into the soil and finished the concoction off with a handful of damp dirt and bits of cold grass.

Matilda placed the bowl on her head. Her brow gathered between her eyes as she desperately tried to recall the words of the spell. Finally, after several tries and plenty of concentration, she composed a complete sentence.

"With the force of good my spirit will rip away from me and fall to the Earth with my soul."

She repeated the sentence three times, each time altering the words ever so slightly, but enough to invoke what she never expected. Afterwards, she removed the bowl from her head and tossed its contents out the window.

Matilda didn't know exactly *how* powerful her words were. What she recited, committed to memory, was not Amando's chant to protect her from witches, but an incantation that affected her very soul, one that stirred and disrupted an absentee guardian angel in a way she never imagined.

That night, a neon cloud illuminated the tip of Finger's Edge. With a roar and blinding flash, a bolt of electricity penetrated the rock and made it glow like a red-hot branding iron. A portion of a cloud ripped away from the sky and fell upon Finger's Edge.

Ben's gaping eyes were glued to the glass of his bedroom window as he watched Finger's Edge disappeared under a glowing vaporous veil.

~

From the window of her Hogan, Dancing Wind observed the same sight. Her eyes were riddled with concern. She knew that such a profound tempest was a sign of a turbulent spirit and to witness its raw power only meant bad luck.

Dancing Wind stayed up all night and prayed. She ground several soft colorful stones into a dust and made a sand painting of the scene she witnessed on her Hogan floor. She chanted songs in a sacred ceremony that cleansed her from a wrathful spirit's affliction and gave her the ability to reason with it.

Matilda's home sat supreme at the top of a hill. The rising sun washed the white stucco ranch house in pink light. That's when Matilda made the discovery.

"Ben!"

Her yell caused the roosters to swallow their bellow. She ran outside and belted out another call.

Ben did not answer. The boy was nowhere to be found under the waking sky. Furiously, she stomped the grounds and stirred the whole ranch awake.

"Get up!" she screamed, "Ben is missing!"

The ranch hands fell out of their beds and stood at attention. Amando pulled up his pants and harnessed the horses, still groggy with sleep. Matilda pranced first to the barn, then to the Hogan where Dancing Wind lived.

"Dancing Wind!" she commanded. "This is all your fault!"

Dancing Wind looked up from her bed. Her eyes questioned the wicked accusation.

"Ben is missing! It's all your stupid stories that caused him to leave!" Matilda's nostrils flared.

"Missing?" Dancing Wind's belly churned with fear.

"Where is he?"

"I don't know!"

Matilda glared at her with dark eyes and thundered away. Dancing Wind slowly stepped outside her home and observed the ensuing chaos. She watched Matilda jump on a horse, startling the poor animal, and ride off with Amando into the vast acres of Big M.

Dancing Wind asked the sun to watch over Ben, wherever he was and to guide him back home safely.

~

Ben dared not look down. He felt his heart drumming in his chest when he reached the top. The red dirt beneath his feet was softer than powder and sprinkled with traces of greenery. The sky was glistening as turquoise. Gnarled trees clung to sparkling stones and its arms stretched skyward to tickle the clouds. *What is all the fuss about*, he wondered as he swam through fat bushes and stepped over slabs of rocks. There was no Great One living up here nor was there any sign of witches.

The breeze disturbed a small creature somewhere. Ben froze. Was there a Raven's nest nearby? Were they the cries of a coyote? Ben heard it again and wondered what kind of life dwelled on the top of the mysterious Finger's Edge. The sun warmed his small shoulders as he followed the sound.

Through curled branches he saw something and stepped closer. A mammoth nest made from intertwined bleached wood was partially hidden in the crevasses of a small cave. Something inside it caused the nest to move. Ben gingerly placed his feet so he wouldn't make a sound. His heart raced as he walked closer and stopped. Something inside it was alive. Tiny hands reached out from the twig cradle. Wrapped in dove feathers, a baby goggled at the sight of Ben, who stared in disbelief. She was beautiful, small and soft with crystal clear blue eyes and jet-black hair. He never saw eyes like hers before. They reflected the sky.

Something made the fine hair on his pink arms stand up. Ben felt an eerie sensation that they were not alone.

He stood still, like Dancing Wind once taught him, and slowly moved his head to look around. There was nothing but a cascade of rusty rocks and twisted branches. A small breeze rustled his hair and he noticed his shadow was gone. Ben looked up. A cloud pilfered the sun.

The gentle breeze grew stronger. Ben heard a voice that made him shiver. This sound didn't belonged to any human being but grew out of the wind. It was a hundred ghostly voices that breathed a single word that poured through the canyons.

"Graaaaccccceeeee."

~

By the time Matilda and Amando searched all one hundred and fifty nine acres of Big M it was late afternoon. There was no sign of Ben. Matilda took one more gallop around the stately house as her bustle bubbled like a parachute behind her big backside. Finding nothing, she dismounted the horse and wearily drudged into the house.

Amando took her horse and his towards the stable, but was halted by the command of her voice before he reached his destination.

"Amando! Send some men to Finger's Edge."

Amando stopped. The giant rock loomed before him like a headstone in the dying sun. No one who had been to this cursed placed ever came back alive. Amando feared for the men he had to send but most of all, he feared for himself. He knew Matilda would make him lead the search party. Amando pleaded, but his desperate words fell futile on deaf ears.

"Amando, MOVE!" she directed.

He took a deep breath and reluctantly began his journey. Matilda went back in the house and slammed the door.

A fire brewed inside her. The evil curse contaminated her thoughts. She marched into her bedroom and fell on her bed. The rusted springs beneath the mattress of her wrought iron bed squashed under her weight. Matilda gazed at the picture of Elmo on her nightstand. The photo was dark and blurry but the face it captured resonated with kindness. She pulled it to her face and stared, as if an answer lied in the photograph's eyes. Her breath fogged the glass.

"Elmo! Don't take him away from me!" Her voice quivered with desperation. "He's all I got left," she squeezed her eyes shut and hung her head. After a quiet moment, she opened her eyes and slammed the photo on the nightstand, which put another dent in the wood. "Elmo," she whispered, "return my son to me, please."

"Matilda!" the far away voice of Amando lingered in the air.

She sucked in her breath, left the room and stepped outside. The flicker of a gas lamp illuminated the distance. Within range of the orange light was a small figure. Matilda rushed towards it.

Ben stood small, meek and dirty in the dim light of the gas lamp. Amando kneeled next to him and wrapped the baby in his jacket.

"Ben!" shouted Matilda when she saw him. The boy stepped back as his angry mother approached. She slapped his face. Amando winced and held his jacket tighter, concealing the evidence.

"Where have you been?"

Ben shrugged, holding his sore cheek. Amando placed a

comforting hand on his little shoulder.

Then Matilda heard it. She moved her ear towards Amando and heard it again. Amando looked back without a word. Matilda moved to Amando, pulled at the jacket in his arms and saw it.

"What is this?" she hissed and looked at Amando, then at Ben.

"Esta un bebé, Señora," Amando answered softly.

"I know that! Where did it come from?" Matilda swiveled to Ben. "Where did it come from?"

Ben scrambled for the correct answer.

"Señora Matilda," interrupted Amando in a pleading, tired tone, "but I have found your son safe, sleeping at the foot of the canyon and –"

"Shut up!" she shouted with her eyes still locked on her son. The baby began to cry and Amando cradled the frightened child.

"Where did you find this?"

His stubby finger unwillingly pointed in the direction of Finger's Edge. Amando's shocked eyes fell on Ben.

"How many times did I tell you never to go there?"

Matilda took her son by the earlobe. He gasped at the sudden move. "Didn't I tell you that's a place for witches?"

"But, it's not!" pleaded Ben.

"Don't talk back!" she shouted and released his ear. Matilda's angry look fell on the squirming baby.

"A witch!" she uttered "Drown it in the well."

Amando stared at Matilda, "But she is only a little baby."

"Do as I say, or else," she threatened as she grabbed Ben's arm and dragged him towards the house.

By the light of the lamp, Amando saw the child's eyes becoming heavy with sleep. Her round, soft face reminded him too much of his own daughter, Juanetta, who died of influenza only a few months earlier. The desert night was cool as he cuddled the child in his warm jacket. Amando rose to his feet, and with a long sigh, walked into the night.

Ben spent that night awake in bed. His bottom was sore from the paddling his mother gave him, but that wasn't the reason for his sleeplessness. His eyes burned with salty liquid when he thought of the baby being tossed into the cold well and breathing water until her body became full as she sunk into her deep, watery grave. It was his fault. Had he never brought the child back, she might still be alive and well in the protection of Finger's Edge's spirits. He was angry with his mother for her stupidity and vowed never to tell her anything again.

~

By the time the sun arose, he was soundly asleep.

Dancing Wind's night was disturbed with strange dreams. In one dream, a giant cloud marbled with gray veins threw bolts of light at her. As she ran from its enraged attacks, the cloud spun in a violent whir and plunged into the river. She awoke in a sweat and by this time it was morning. Perhaps it was the after affects of the lightening spirit that caused her to dream such a thing.

She looked out the window. The clouds were round and solid and tan as flesh. They gathered in a circle, like a halo above the tip of Finger's Edge. She wondered if the Cloud People were trying to tell her something.

The dream catcher above her bed was tangled, its feathers caught in a knot within its web. Dancing Wind removed it from the rusted nail and shook it free. As she did this, she heard a Raven's greeting, so she hawked back. She heard it again. It was not a Raven's cry but a sound she had not heard in many years.

Dancing Wind opened the creaking door of the Hogan. The morning light spilled in along with the sound. Dancing Wind stepped outside and found its source.

An unusual bundle sat just beyond her doorstep. Dancing Wind approached it carefully and saw the baby crying inside. Lines grew across her face as she reached her weathered hands to lift the sweet baby.

Dancing Wind tried to find the correlation between her dream and this unusual event. Cradling the baby, she looked to Finger's Edge, standing peacefully on the horizon. It was a soothing comfort to her.

"O Great Spirit of the sky and land, thank you for this small soul."

A breeze freed a strand from her gray braided bun. Dancing Wind drank in the smooth air and moved her head to the West. Holding the infant in her aged arms, she closed her eyes and uttered, "*Ahéhee'*."

CHAPTER THREE

Although Ben's punishment required him to stay indoors all day, he managed to escape. He had to find solace and comfort, and there was only one place to go. The way to outsmart his mother was to quietly sneak out the bedroom window and scale down the side of the house. The climb to Finger's Edge gave him the courage to do this.

The boy followed the worn familiar trail to the Hogan near the barn, where he heard the cows lowing. Ben blinked in disbelief at what he saw in Dancing Wind's arms. The baby suckled from a cow's udder.

"Ben!" she smiled softly. " I am so happy you are home safe."

Ben still gaped in amazement.

"The baby," he whispered as Dancing Wind removed the contented baby from the cow, coddled the child on her chest and tapped her back gently.

"This morning she waits for me outside my door. A gift from the Great Spirit." The old woman glowed.

Ben looked at Dancing Wind, not knowing how to respond. Dancing Wind noted the confusion on Ben's face and patiently waited for him to speak.

"I found her," he began as Dancing Wind leaned curiously closer. "I found her, but my mother told Amando to drown her."

"Why?" Dancing Wind's brow wrinkled, although nothing Matilda said or did surprised her.

"Because," said Ben as he meekly touched the baby's hand. "Because my mother said she's a witch."

Dancing Wind shook her head. "The only witch your mother should fear is herself," she said as she put the sleeping child onto a small pile of cloth covered hay. "Where did you find her?"

"At Finger's Edge."

Dancing Wind stared at Ben.

"Finger's Edge?" she repeated to herself. "You went there?"

Ben nodded. Dancing Wind looked at him, at the slumbering babe, then at him again.

"Are you mad at me?" Ben was nervous. He knew how Dancing Wind felt about the sacred towering butte. "I'm sorry."

"No, no," she shook her head. A wild rush shot through her body, an excitement usually reserved for youth. Her heart pounded at the thought that her destiny was about to be fulfilled.

"It was so beautiful, Dancing Wind, there are curly trees and fat cacti and blue flowers and soft dirt. That's where I found her, in a nest near a little cave."

Dancing Wind listened carefully.

Ben told her about the mysterious cloud and the strange sensation that made him feel he wasn't alone. When he spoke of the wind, Dancing Wind leaned closer still.

"It sounded like a million voices. But at the same time, it was only one voice. And it said a word: Grrraaaaaaccccccceeeeee."

"Grace," whispered Dancing Wind. "Grace."

Ben looked to the old woman for the meaning of the strange phenomena.

"Ben, you are blessed." She beamed at him proudly. "The Great Spirit called you to find this child for me."

Ben thought Dancing Wind was about to cry, but no tears came from her gleaming eyes.

"BEN!" a shrill voice pierced the soothing moment.

Ben jumped and before Dancing Wind could conceal the child, Matilda darkened the doorway.

"Ben!" she charged, "You are punished today! Get out of here!" Her fast eyes dug out the secret. "And what's *that* doing here?" She pointed at the baby. Ben trembled.

"Get rid of that thing!" she ordered Dancing Wind. "Now!"

Dancing Wind's eyes quietly fell upon the baby, then soared to Matilda.

"I see no *thing* to get rid of."

"That witch!" Her thundering roar caused the baby to cry.

"There is no witch here, Miss Matilda." Dancing Wind gently comforted the baby in her arms.

"Get rid of that wicked baby!"

"If harm comes to her, Great Spirit will be angry with you."

Tension mounted between Dancing Wind and Matilda as Ben watched his worlds collide.

"AMANDO!" She yelled at the top of her lungs. Her voice carried through the acres of the ranch and bounced off all the buttes and mesas until it wrangled its victim. Dancing Wind quietly added one more thing.

"If this child goes, I go."

Matilda caught her words before they fell out of her mouth. She knew what Dancing Wind was worth. With the ranch on a steady decline and short two ranch hands, Matilda relied heavily on this experienced and invaluable employee. Dancing Wind was the only worker on the ranch who never took pay. Instead, she worked out of a promise to Elmo, a concept Matilda never understood.

When Amando arrived, he knew what Matilda discovered.

"Amando! Why is this child here and not in the well?"

"But Señora Matilda, I did as you said. I do not know how this child has arrived here!" He took a cigarette from his pocket and lit up. "You know, I heard it said that it is severe bad luck to drown a witch." He took a few puffs in the pronounced pause that commonly preceded one of his tales then blew a cloud of smoke. "I believe it is good the child refused to drown. I say this niña bruja has spared you."

The news silenced her. Amando knew her all too well. She stared at him with a frown and bit the inside of her mouth. He adjusted his sombrero and took another drag.

"Forgive me, Señora, but I have much work to do." He gave her a short smile, winked at Ben and left. Matilda looked at Dancing Wind, the baby and Ben and took a deep, loud breath.

"I don't ever want to see that child come anywhere near me, my house or my son!"

His mother's last word echoed in Ben's ear.

"Ben, you come with me. Today, you are punished!" She dragged Ben out the door.

~

Dancing Wind noticed the same unusual cloud formation hovering above Finger's Edge for four days in a row. She was not the only one who made this observation. Neighboring Navajos saw it too and knew what it meant. They followed their hearts to find the place where the baby was and arrived secretly at Dancing Wind's door to pay quiet homage to the little One called *Grace Of The Clouds*.

The Navajos knew of Dancing Wind's legacy and came to bring a blessing. A Navajo man placed a turquoise necklace with a small hide pouch around Dancing Wind's wrinkled neck. The bag was filled with sacred stones, prayers and herbs. The man told Dancing Wind it was a medicine to protect, strengthen and guide her in the new challenge she was about to face. Dancing Wind smiled graciously and held the child close.

They also hoped to see the boy, the only one to their knowledge, the Great Spirits had allowed to behold their sacred grounds. Dancing Wind promised to introduce them.

One hot afternoon, Ben planned his rendezvous. It was the day Matilda and Amando took the buggy into the city for business and left Ben under the supervision of Amando's wife.

It wouldn't be difficult to disappear for a while. Rosa didn't care what Ben did and Ben usually didn't like staying there because he hated Juan. Juan was a spoiled brat who made fun of him and played nasty tricks. There was something about Juan that was just downright evil.

As Ben watched his mother pull away in a cloud of beige dust, he was distracted by the ensuing chaos behind him.

"Juan! ¿Que pasa?" The weight of Rosa's fat body hammered the shrieking floorboards as she chased her deviant son. "Juan! Put that back! Ora! Est cigarettes de su padre! Juan! Stop!"

Juan dashed by, teasing his mother with a wicked laugh.

When he caught Ben staring at him, Juan snarled, making the ugliest face Ben ever saw. With one swift motion, Juan plucked an egg from his pocket and hurled it at Ben.

It cracked in Ben's hair and dripped down his face. Ben didn't know it, but his nostrils were flaring and his face was red. He didn't hear the roar that came from his throat as he charged the laughing boy, on impulse. Their scuffle didn't last long before Rosa kicked Ben out of her house.

This made Ben's plan go even smoother. When he arrived at the Hogan to meet Dancing Wind, he found a small gathering waiting for him. The Indians wanted to touch him, talk to him and hear first hand about Finger's Edge. As he entered, seven people smiled with eager eyes. He felt like a hero. Nervously, he wiped the sticky hair away from his face and looked to Dancing Wind who held Grace on her lap. Dancing Wind smiled and spoke in a language Ben only heard in her songs.

"This is Ben Zander," she said in Navajo.

A woman with very long, dark hair spoke with unfamiliar words. Ben looked at Dancing Wind, who answered the woman.

"She says you are the son of the Brave White Warrior," Dancing Wind translated. Ben looked at her curiously, then at the woman as Dancing Wind continued.

"She says she wants to hear about Finger's Edge."

Ben smiled politely and didn't know how to respond to the question. He felt strange speaking words he knew they wouldn't understand, but Dancing Wind urged him to go on, to tell in his own words what his eyes beheld. And Ben did so. He told them of the gnarled trees whose fingers tickled turquoise the sky. He told them of the soft dirt, shimmering rocks and blue flowers that studded the vivid landscape. He told them about the small cloud that claimed the sun and stole his shadow. When he spoke of the voice in the wind, he drew the crowd closer.

Someone said it was the voice of the Great Spirit that spoke to Ben. Dancing Wind smiled proudly at him and stroked his hair. He grinned awkwardly at the crowd of strangers who gaped.

A small boy with long hair stood up from the group and spoke.

"He says his name is Dark Horse," Dancing Wind translated as the boy spoke, stepping closer, "and he is the son of a great warrior."

The boy took Ben's hand and pressed something into his palm. The object, an arrowhead with its end wrapped in tan fur, hurt. Ben yelled out in pain. The boy held Ben's hand tightly, placed the arrowhead flat in his sore palm and closed his fingers around it. He said something in a musical voice. Ben looked to Dancing Wind again.

"He says you are brave. This arrow is from his father, who died with courage. It is a token of brotherhood."

Ben listened to Dancing Wind's interpretation. The boy spoke again.

"He says this pain is to remind you that you are a warrior, it is for protection." The boy locked his black eyes with Ben's and gave him a nod of friendship. Someone in the crowd called his name and Dark Horse returned to a seat next to his mother.

No one heard the sinister laughter that spilled from Juan's lips as he peeked in the window. Unaware they were being watched the Indians all gathered closer to the child, spoiling her and Ben with attention and wonder. Juan knew exactly what he was going to do.

When the Indians took all they had seen and heard home to their families, they didn't know this was their last visit.

Juan's news of the event quickly reached Matilda's ears, who immediately placed two armed ranch hands at the borders of Big M with orders to shoot any trespassers.

Ben was not allowed to visit Dancing Wind's Hogan again. This time, Matilda would make certain of it.

CHAPTER FOUR

It was first noticed in the barn. The chickens laid more eggs, the pigs got fatter and the cows sprouted forth more milk. Mysteriously too, the weather was always perfect. The rain instantly quenched the land before it had the chance to cry out with thirst. The wind blew at just the right speed to insure a proper and healthy dissemination of seeds. When it was too hot, a cloud arrived to cast a cool shadow. The harvest was like none ever seen on Big M. For the first time, there was vegetation on the land. Fruits and vegetables grew hearty, with crops yielding five times their normal amount. The cattle quadrupled its size and each animal doubled its weight. Sheep were fat with wool. No one understood why these things were happening, but no one questioned it either. Matilda just assumed it was her luck finally changing for the better.

The child with hair black as night and eyes of the sky, grew to be extraordinary. When she was still a toddler, Dancing Wind observed her quietly conversing with the sky. Once, she even saw the child demand rain from out of a clear blue and the sky obeyed, offering sheets of showers, which sent Matilda running for shelter like a mad woman. Dancing Wind smiled in wonderment, convinced who the little girl named Grace really was.

Although Matilda had banned all visits from the Navajos, on a few occasions, Dancing Wind noticed Dark Horse in the nearby shrubbery, discretely watching. The boy studied with the deer and knew how to move so not a single ear would hear him. Dancing Wind kept a watchful eye to be sure no harm came to the curious boy.

Little Grace was a great help to Dancing Wind. She instinctively knew the land and assisted with every chore. She fed the animals, cleaned the stalls, milked the cows, collected the eggs, turned the soil, cared for the farm, washed the laundry and hung them to dry. All these things came naturally to the six-year-old, who was born with a special gift.

Occasionally Grace noticed the boy who lived in the big, white house. Though she only saw him from a distance, she sensed a connection and innately liked him. She knew his name was Ben and his mother was nasty. Grace found a place in her small heart to have pity on the ugly woman who governed the land. No one spoke to Grace except for Dancing Wind and sometimes Amando, who came to deliver orders from Señora Matilda. For some reason, "the man with the big dirty hat," as she came to know him, seemed to have a strange reverence for her. He was always nice to her, but she sensed his discomfort in her presence.

Dancing Wind set up a small bed of hay and sheep's skin for Grace. On many nights, Grace stayed outside, captivated by the many stars that infested the night sky. Dancing Wind told her they were the thousand eyes of her ancestors that kept close watch on everyone through the night.

Grace liked the idea of being watched by the iridescent twinkles. It made her feel comfortable, protected and loved.

"Go to sleep, Grace," Dancing Wind beckoned her gently.

Grace had to pry herself from the studded sky and go inside, to the soft bed made of chicken feathers and covered by sheepskin. She slipped under the covers and snuggled in. A small flame dancing in an iron kettle kept the dwelling both warm and lit. Grace watched Dancing Wind slowly ease down on her own bed in the orange light. Her moves were deliberate and patient. The bed made a quiet crunching sound as her weight sank into the bed.

"Din?" As Grace called her. "Who am I?"

She was as graceful as her name. Dancing Wind looked at the child whose face shimmered in the light and more lines gathered around Dancing Wind's smile.

"Din? Where did I come from?" Grace was eager and serious, her eyes were blue crystals reflecting the flame. Dancing Wind froze in place and looked at the hungry eyes across from her, so innocent yet so wise. Grace rested her small face in her hand and relaxed, waiting for the honey voice to unravel a tale.

"You come from the clouds," she said and paused to gaze at a jumping piece of fire, "and you come from the dirt." Dancing Wind took a deep breath and spoke in a voice that melted butter.

"My little one, you were born in a great place, on a sacred rock, where only Cloud People live." She pointed her finger west. "On top of Finger's Edge."

Grace hung on the warm words, swallowing and ingesting them whole. She knew all about Finger's Edge. The history of the grand rock was one of the stories that sent her to slumber each night. Grace wondered if Din was telling her a new tale. She sat still and listened.

"A boy, a brave boy, found you where your mother and father left you. And he brought you to me, to watch over, to guide and to grow you."

Dancing Wind watched the girl's face absorb the news.

"Who is the boy?"

"You know who he is, Grace. The boy who always smiles at you – the boy you like."

"Ben?" she said with a gleeful start. She knew there was something she liked about him.

"Then, who is my mother and my father?"

"Mother Earth and Father Sky," she said with a remnant of a dimple, knowing she was repeating herself.

Grace's dark, thin eyebrows scuffled in confusion, but she did not ask again. As far as she knew, Din was her mother and father, the only parent she ever knew. But Ben – she must talk to Ben tomorrow. She wanted to know who he was and why he found her. Grace fell asleep with a smile. Dancing Wind looked at her for just a moment longer before she closed her eyes too.

~

Matilda made more and more trips to the city. The produce of Big M was in sudden demand. The town in turn anticipated Matilda's visits with mixed feelings. On the one hand, they looked forward to her arrival with glee, knowing she was bringing bountiful baskets of the finest vegetables and fruits they had seen. Corn the size of broom handles. Mushrooms as big as boulders. Sweet potatoes with a one-foot circumference. Eyes popped and hands grabbed at the heartiest crop ever indulged. Produce moved off the shelves faster than they were replaced. Stores were busy. Money was flowing. Merchants were happy.

On the other hand, they dreaded Matilda'a snippy remarks, her offensive appearance, and her vibrating roar which made cowboys shake in their boots. With all of that came a hard bargain. Matilda demanded top dollar for her goods and usually got it.

Her newfound wealth enabled her to do many things: hire more ranch hands to handle the abundance of cattle, buy new items for the house and even hire a housekeeper who also cared for Ben while she was away.

Whatever Matilda had done, her luck seemed to change. She attributed it to the spell Amando gave her six years ago, which was still working. She was sure all the witches, with the exception of Grace, were gone from her life. The curse was finally gone.

"Amando," she began as they rode back. "Fire Dancing Wind."

Amando looked at Matilda with puzzled eyes.

"And tell her to take the little witch with her." She counted the dollars in her hands.

Amando shook his head. "I would not do such a thing, if I were you, Señora. It is bad luck." His hat flapped slightly in the breeze.

"My luck is good now. That potion worked." She counted the last of the dollars.

Amando pulled on the reins and the horses stopped.

"When did you use it?"

"Amando, why are you stopping! Continue!"

"When did you use it?"

"Six years ago." She folded the money into a pouch wrapped around her waist. "And see? My luck is good."

Amando looked at her suspiciously. "Did you say the right words, Señora?"

Matilda's nostrils flared. "Of course!" she spit out. "Can't you see all the good luck around you, you foolish Mexican! Now, Hurry up, let's GO!"

Amando shook his head and snapped the reins. The horses continued.

"Sometimes," he said as he stared at the road ahead of him, "if you say it wrong, something else will happen instead. It is very dangerous."

"Shut up and drive."

~

Maria was stern, short and fat. She had little patience for dirty kitchens or misbehaved children, like Ben who had become more and more unmanageable by the day. Ben smeared the entire kitchen with mud and horse dung, making Maria red with furry. She pulled his hair and locked him in his room.

"Benyamanos! Diabalos!" she screamed some obscenities in Spanish and held the apron to her nose.

Little did she know, Maria played right into his plans.

In his room, he attached a piece of paper next to an open window. The breeze made it sound like he was flipping through books. He fussed with the lock on his closet door so it squeaked open, slammed shut with the wind and moved his bed in front of the door.

Ben was gone. From now on, he decided nothing would keep him from seeing Grace. He *had* to see her. He missed talking to Dancing Wind. Although the past six years were filled with school, studies, chores and Maria, he never forgot his only friend and *his* baby, whom he watched grow from a distance.

The familiar scent of chickens, the vague smell of sour milk, the sweet odor of dry hay erased the vacant years away from Dancing Wind's home. Ben peeked in the Hogan. Nobody was home. He scanned the horizon, rows of endless green, fruit trees and large vegetables saturated the once-ill land. The small farm was bursting with animal activity and sounds. He felt a touch on his back and instantly turned around.

Grace smiled at him. Her crystal eyes and flowing black hair dazzled him.

"Ben!" she said in a jubilant voice. He heard a trace of Dancing Wind's accent in her words. "I waited for you. I knew you were coming."

She warmed him in a charming way.

"The wind told me." She was eager and welcoming. A tingle crawled along his arms. His heart floated.

"The wind," he repeated softly, his face flushed. "Grace?"

She pulled his hand. "Come with me."

She seemed far older than her mere six years. Ben revered her, yet felt protective over her. He followed Grace to the field where he saw Dancing Wind herding a flock of sheep. When she saw him, her face lit up, she dropped her walking stick and opened her arms. Ben never imagined more lines could find a place on her brittle skin, but they did. A hundred more rippled with her smile. Ben ran to her embrace.

"Ben!" she busted and wrapped her arms around the boy.

"Dancing Wind!" His heart fluttered.

The feeling here was good. He had forgotten how positive and peaceful it was at Dancing Wind's Hogan. What a difference from what he felt in his home. His mother was a tyrant and had become increasingly more so with her new wealth. It made her arrogant.

Ben decided he was going to stay here, with Dancing Wind and Grace, forever.

~

The stench of dung instantly hit Matilda as she stepped into the house. Her presence interrupted Maria's frenzied cleaning. Maria turned to her with an ignited face.

"Ai! Señora! Su Benyamanos es diabalo, Señora!" Maria spit out the words frantically, sparing no time in telling Matilda about the rebellious behavior of her spoiled son.

"American! Talk American to me!" Matilda hated it when people spoke Spanish to her. She considered herself an American, since she was married to one.

"Benyamin! He put all yis mess around here."

Matilda listened with a furrowed brow before she marched up to his room and banged on the door. She heard the sounds from within the locked room, the paper fluttering, the door slamming with a rhythmic beat. She knew her son all too well. She turned on her heels and stomped down the stairs, grabbed a gas lamp, and flew out the door. The sky was painted with purples and reds. The sun was already absent. She pranced to the back of the house and saw Ben's open window. Matilda let out a fiery breath, marched through the fields to Dancing Wind's Hogan and kicked the door open.

The bolt startled the three huddled around a center golden fire, eating a vegetable stew from a stone pot. Matilda's face was a jack-o-lantern in the orange light.

"Ben!" she roared, blowing his hair back. A trace of fear glistened in his brown eyes. There was uncomfortable silence. Dancing Wind stirred the soup calmly and silently watched the woman in the doorway. This was the first time Grace saw Matilda up close. She studied Matilda's hot face and decided she wasn't afraid.

"You hungry?" Grace asked boldly.

Ben's eyes flew to Grace, then to his mother, who quickly glanced at the child.

"Ben! Get up and come with me," she spoke through clenched teeth.

Ben's legs slowly obeyed the fearsome voice though his heart didn't want to listen. His body was a helpless soldier to his mother's commands. He wanted to scream out, but he found no voice in his throat, just a trembling weakness that squeezed his voice box. He heard Dancing Wind's quiet voice telling him to go with his mother.

"Dancing Wind! What did I tell you! We had a deal!"

Dancing Wind looked at the towering woman calmly as she poured a ladle of thick soup into a wooden dish.

"I kept my end of your deal." She placed the bowl in front of Grace who watched the theatrical scenario unfold.

Matilda's tone was snide and sarcastic. "Pack your bags, you and that little witch. I don't need you anymore!"

"NO!" Ben heard his voice scream. Matilda looked at her son as if he were a stranger. Tears of fear lined his eyes and a hot tingle danced across his forehead.

"If you force them to leave, I swear, Mother, I will run away from you forever." Matilda slapped his face.

"Now you're talking stupid, boy." She gripped his arm and looked at Dancing Wind. "Tomorrow is your last day here." With those words, she vanished, pulling a humiliated Ben behind her.

Dancing Wind sat in silence for a minute. The ladle seeped inside the thick brew, and slowly sunk to the bottom. Grace looked at her.

"Din. She can't do that. This is our home."

Dancing Wind looked at her and blinked her eyes slowly.

"Grace, the land is our sister. The sky is our brother. Anywhere we go is home." Her smooth smile gave little Grace great comfort.

It would be hard to leave. Dancing Wind never broke a promise in her life, but this was one she hoped Elmo's spirit would understand. She really had no choice.

When morning came, Grace found Dancing Wind sitting on the ground, with her face towards the rising sun and her eyes closed. She quietly kneeled in the wet grass beside her.

"Grace," Dancing Wind said softly, without moving, without opening her eyes. "Close your eyes and feel the wind. Listen."

The wind rustled through the trees lightly with a gentle sigh. "The wind tells us what to do. Listen."

Grace sat quietly with her eyes closed and listened. She held her breath for a moment so the sound of her breathing wouldn't interfere with the faint whispering of the breeze. She listened and concentrated.

"Din, everything will be okay. Wind said so."

A meager but proud smile found itself on Dancing Wind's lips. The tension in her forehead melted.

"What did she say?"

With a small pause, Grace replied, "She says we go, but we come back." Grace opened her eyes and saw Dancing Wind staring at her.

A Raven flew overhead with a greeting. Dancing Wind knew it was a sign that all would be well. She answered the bird's squawk and watched it become a speck in sky.

~

There was a knock.

Matilda opened the large oak door and saw Joseph, her neighbor and owner of the small ranch bordering Big M. Joseph Kilbee bought the land just about a year ago and was struggling to make ends meet.

The young man nervously removed his worn, flimsy hat and tried to hide his initial fright when she opened the door. He saw Matilda only from a distance and had no idea exactly how offensive she really was. He feigned a smile.

"Mrs. Zander, good morning." He was polite though his trembling hat revealed his true feelings.

"It's afternoon," she retorted without the slightest trace of a smile. "May I come in?"

Matilda examined him closely. She opened the door and stepped outside.

"What is it you want, Kilbee?" She addressed him sternly, folding her arms across her broad chest. Her rancid breath forced him to take a step back.

"Well," he lowered his eyes for a moment, "I, well, own that little spread over there." He pointed Southwest. Matilda locked her eyes on his face.

"So?"

"Well, Matilda, uh, Mrs. Zander, things have been really hard for us. We have no ranch hands, we can't afford them, and I heard that, well..."

"Get to the point, Kilbee."

He took a deep breath. "Okay. I understand you fired your Indian helper. I was just wondering if I could..."

"Word travels fast, doesn't it?"

"I guess it does. So. Could I hire her? I mean, could you tell me where I can find her?"

Matilda leaned closer and squinted. "Why do you want to hire that old woman? She's just about ready to die."

Joseph shook his head in small jerky moves, as if his neck was on a spring. "I heard she's good. She can really grow stuff. It's all over town, that she and that kid, she can work magic with the land. And she works for free. Please, Mrs. Zander, tell me where she is."

Matilda bit the inside of her mouth. "What else do you hear in town, Kilbee?"

He shook his head nervously again. "Well, that the product you bring is the finest ever. Even your livestock is the leanest. And you never had that kind of product before that kid joined the old Indian. Everybody knows it. It's all over. Please, tell me..."

"No!" she blasted. "It isn't because of that little witch, and she *is* one, you know. And it isn't because of that ancient fat Indian. It's because of *me!*" She shouted into his ear. "Do you understand? It's *my* luck that's changed. That's why my product is the finest. It's *me!* Do you understand? Make sure you tell everybody that. You hear?"

"Okay, okay," he nodded quickly, "But please tell me where Dancing Wind is. I need the help desperately. *Please!*"

Matilda shook her head with a scowl. "How should I know? Go find her yourself and you'll see how much heartache that witch will bring you!" She inhaled noisily. "Good day, Kilbee."

Matilda stepped inside the house and slammed the door on his face. All this news swished around inside her thick skull. She poured a cup of hot steaming coffee and threw the boiling beverage down her throat like a shot of whisky. She sighed loudly, staring off in the distance as remnant steam rose from her mouth.

Upstairs, her son was very busy. He removed the sheet from his bed and tossed every valuable thing he could think of in the center of it – clothes, books, some favorite rocks. His put his most cherished thing – his good luck arrow – in his pocket.

He folded the sheet up and knotted the ends into a convenient handle. He looked to his window. It was nailed shut. Since Matilda kept all doors on the second floor locked, Ben had no choice but to walk right by his mother downstairs. He felt the sharp edge of the arrow in his pocket, a reminder to stay strong and be courageous. He walked down the steps and through the kitchen.

Matilda's thoughts were broken at the sight of her son walking by with a large, white bundle in tow.

"Where are you going?"

He did not respond. Matilda rose from her chair as Ben opened the door. She followed him.

"Benjamin!" she yelled. "Stop!" He felt his feet obey.

"Where are you going?"

"Away!" he shouted back. "I'm running far away from you. You took away everything from me! My only friends are gone and I hate you."

There was fire in Matilda's eyes.

"Stupid! Nobody's your friend. Don't you know that by now? Nobody! As soon as they learn about your curse, nobody will ever be your friend!"

Ben felt a hot tear stream down his cheek.

"No! You're stupid! You and your curse!"

Ben imagined he saw flames shooting from her nostrils as she charged at him like a bull. "You don't talk to me that way!"

Ben found his feet fleeing, for once they disobeyed her and obliged him. They flew and carried him for miles. Matilda, with her large legs and heavy physique, found no way to catch up to her scurrying son. He looked back and saw his mother in the far distance. He could feel her rage, but didn't care.

~

Dancing Wind and Grace made a small campsite near the Navajo reservation on the northern outskirts of Big M. When Dark Horse found their camp, he supplied them with food and invited them to his home where they gathered with friends. They sat around a fire for hours as they listened to Dancing Wind's stories. But Dark Horse and his friends were mostly intrigued by the little one called Grace. They marveled at her eyes, her wisdom and the story of her birth.

Ben knew exactly where to find them. When he arrived at their campsite, Dark Horse immediately recognized his friend and welcomed Ben into his home with a warm embrace.

~

Five days was enough time for Matilda to do what she had to. At first, she didn't care about Ben. *He'll see*, she thought to herself. The boy had to learn a lesson. She wondered how her son turned out to be such a brat. *How? It is part of the curse*, she thought, *to have such a mischievous child.*

By the end of the fifth day, she began to feel his absence. By the end of this day, she arrived at some other conclusions as well.

For five days, her ranch hands complained about the barn. The cows didn't have any milk. The chickens neither ate nor laid a single egg. The ground bore no new vegetables and the fruits rotted over night and fell to the ground. Matilda shook her head. She hated to be at the mercy of anyone.

"Buenos dias, Señora." Amando, removed his giant sombrero as he entered the house and took a chair from the table. The wood creaked as he sat next to her and quietly removed his sombrero. Matilda looked at the dark, sincere eyes that peeked out from his tan, weathered face. Juan was nothing like him, she thought to herself, he was tall, thin and slithery – a troublemaker. The teenager was new on the payroll and she already couldn't trust him.

"What is it, Amando?" Her voice was somber and drained of it usual fury.

"It is five days now we have no eggs." He looked at the hat in his hands. Matilda's eyes were hot on him.

"And the cows too, are dry." Amando looked up at her. "And Señora, even the vegetables..."

"Stop!" The voice belched smoke, then hushed to a soft steam whisper, "please."

Amando felt a sudden rush of compassion. "Señora, if you will," he said quietly, "may I make a suggestion?"

Matilda studied the details of his weary face and waited.

"I must say this." His pause was one of sincere hesitation. He looked at his hat again. "I must suggest the return of the niña bruja."

Matilda's nose expanded. Her lips pursed, making her mustache appear thicker. She couldn't help but think about Kilbee and the townspeople. Although she didn't believe any of it, today, she considered the possibility of its truth. She thought of her son and had no idea where he was or where the Indian and the witch were. She thought about her luck. Perhaps the curse had a sinister sense of humor that fooled her into believing it changed. Perhaps the little witch put a spell on the ranch as revenge for how Matilda treated her. She wondered if Ben was in trouble and if he was eating all right.

"The witch has taken my son from me." Her voice was tired. "You must be careful of the witch."

Amando grinned reassuringly, "No worry, Señora, I will bring my son Juan with me, and that will neutralize the witch's power." He put his hat back on his head and nodded eagerly. "No worry. She is not a bad witch. I have seen worse."

He lit up a cigarette and let the smoke billow from out of his mouth in a stream that rose to its familiar place on the brim of his hat. Matilda looked at him wearily and saw a tale taking flesh.

"Amando, no stories today, please. Just go."

CHAPTER FIVE

Six years went by and once again Big M thrived. Matilda still refused to speak to Grace or Dancing Wind and made Maria the liaison between the barn and herself.

When Dancing Wind and Grace returned quietly to their post on Big M, Matilda realized there wasn't anything she could do to keep Ben away from them. Reluctantly, she accepted this, since this was the only way he would live under her roof. She insisted that Ben wear a blessed medallion, took a silver crucifix, dipped it in holy water and put the heavy chain around his neck. Ben promised to wear it. He didn't care what he had to do, as long as he could be with his friends.

Grace grew more beautiful by the day. She was almost thirteen and on the brink of adulthood. Her long, velvety black hair flowed to her waist from beneath the worn cowboy hat she got from Ben. Her eyes were glistening gems. Ben was mesmerized. From a window or behind a tree, he watched her secretly, captivated by Grace's every move.

In the afternoons, after school, Ben met her at a secret hideaway, a shallow cave formed by the red rocks at the foot of Finger's Edge. He read to her. Stories of love. Stories of courage, war, and history. He whispered sonnets from yearning lovers and recited poems of nature. Although these fables were so much different than the Navajo stories Dancing Wind told, still, she absorbed them until the sun burned away and it was too dark to read. The cave was their secret place, a magical spot where they spoke to stars, shared their dreams, hopes and fears. So many times Ben wanted to kiss her, hold her, and touch her, but was afraid to. She was so young, but so beautiful. He would have to wait.

"Love looks not with the eyes, but with the mind..." Ben read from a thick book in the escaping light, "And therefore it is winged Cupid ...." he looked up from the yellowing pages to catch Grace's sparkling eyes, watching his lips form sentences she didn't fully understand. Ben tried to read her eyes in a passing moment of awkward silence, then continued.

"...Painted blind – Shakespeare..."

The words softly slipped from his lips. His gaze was unbroken. He shut the book with a thump that echoed his heart. Grace understood and lowered her eyes uncomfortably.

"It's getting late," she whispered, "Dancing Wind will worry."

Quietly, he stood up and shyly reached for her hand. She took it and they walked out of the cave, into the dissolving day, listening to the crunching earth beneath their feet. Neither of them spoke a word.

Ben knew he was hopelessly in love.

And so did his mother.

She recognized the twinkle in her son's eye. *This is going too far*, she thought. She couldn't let her son be trapped by a witch. *No.* She sent Maria to the barn with a command.

Maria's apron was a permanent fixture around her waist. She used it for cooking, cleaning and as protection against the smell of livestock in the barn. She held the stained white-frilled cloth to her nose as she stepped in.

"Buenos dias. Por mañana, Señora Matilda needs more clothes washed." Maria couldn't help but find herself enchanted as well by the clear blue eyes. She recited her list in a nasal voice.

"More baskets of eggs, potatoes and corn preparar por mañana afternoon."

Grace nodded patiently, listening to the list of chores and taking mental note as she milked the cows. Dancing Wind quietly shook her head as she collected loose feathers from the chickens and placed them in a bag.

"Also, she wants you to pluck unos pollo por dinner and pick two bunches of flowers por la casa."

Grace's eyebrows raised curiously at what seemed to be an ambitious task.

"I be back mañana por all these. Someone will bring you clothes soon."

Maria took a slight bow with the apron still adhered to her nose.

"Mucho gracias. Adiós." She stepped out of the barn.

"Matilda," Dancing Wind uttered under her breath.

"What, Din?"

"Matilda, Matilda." She shook her head. "She works you like a slave to keep you away from her son."

"Why?"

"She is afraid of you. She thinks you are a witch."

"But why? What have I done but work hard and do well for her ranch?"

"I do not know, my Grace. People have beliefs and you can not change them." She put the last few feathers in the bag. "You are different from Matilda and from many people. People do not accept those who not like themselves," she sighed wearily.

Dancing Wind placed the bag of feathers down and sat for a minute, resting her tired, old body. Grace sat down beside her.

"My father once said we are all like the sticks of a teepee," she began in a hushed voice. Grace folded her hands to her chin and listened.

"At the bottom, it looks like we are far apart and alone," Dancing Wind outstretched her arms, still holding a few white feathers in her fist. "But when we lift our eyes, we see at the top, all sticks touch. Like sticks of a Tipi, we cannot stand without each other."

Footsteps intruded on their conversation. Juan entered the barn noisily with bundles of dirty clothes in a small, wooden barrow. He leered at Grace and his eyes violated her entire body. Grace felt naked in front of him and folded her arms across her budding breasts. Dancing Wind kept silent watch.

"Leave it there," Grace said to him.

He grinned smugly. "You want any help?" His beady brown eyes said something she did not like. She shook her head and took the wagon into the barn. Juan lingered longer than he had to, staring at her as she ignored him.

"You go now," commanded Dancing Wind in a firm tone. His eyes slid to her and he slithered away from the door.

"I don't like him, Din," she whispered, "he has an evil spirit."

Dancing Wind continued to collect the old feathers and sheep wool tumbling around the barn. As Grace quietly sorted the clothes, she began to feel something. The familiar feeling started in the pit of her stomach and made its way north to her heart, shooting a thousand pins and needles before it squeezed her throat. A tingle seized her legs and her arms and every division of her spine, crawling into her ears. She knew this feeling. It came and went, like the dreams did. But this time the feeling was so overwhelming, it brought her to her knees between piles of Matilda's smelly clothes. Grace had an urge to go outside.

Dancing Wind watched her get up and leave the barn suddenly.

~

Even if Ben looked up, he would not have seen what Grace saw at that moment. He was too busy picking the most attractive wild flowers he could find to surprise Grace.

Finger's Edge stood strangely luminous. Wafting clouds swirled in soupy movements, like a thick steam rushing from a hot fire. Electrified, it flashed white light over the tip of the mountain when everywhere else was blue and pleasant, except for the sky over Finger's Edge. Grace stared at the steel blue cloud and saw something.

It was there, then it was gone.

From out of the massive swells of vapor, she imagined a face – giant, broad and handsome, there at the edge of her consciousness, flickering, then disappearing in a twist of cloud puffs. She blinked her eyes a few times until the face evaporated in the twist of deep blue puffs. Not a trace of the ghostly image remained. She concentrated and stared, picturing the magnificent face, desperate to see it again, but it was impossibly gone. Who was the man she saw in the clouds? The violent action of volatile clouds subsided into an innocent baby blue puff. The image came and went like a dream. Grace wondered if it was.

The encounter left her feeling strangely empty. It was then when she realized for the first time that a huge chunk of her being was missing. There was a space in her chest where her heart used to be – as if her spirit grew wings and flew away. She took a deep breath and filled her lungs with air she held captive for a moment until she slowly let it free. Still entranced, she took her eyes from the looming sacred butte and returned to her chores.

When Ben found her by the river with a wagon of clothes, he noticed something was wrong. He offered her the flowers and she took them without a smile or acknowledgment. Ben looked at her.

"What's the matter?"

Her eyes were locked in a stare, her mind preoccupied with an image and her heart fluttered with uncertainty. She broke her trance.

"Oh. I'm sorry, Ben. Thank you for the help. Your mother needs one more."

"What are you talking about? The flowers are for you."

"Oh. Thank you," she said indifferently.

"Are you okay? Did something happen?"

She shook her head and wished he would go away. She needed to be by herself right now. Ben's nostrils suddenly flared, a trait he unknowingly inherited from his mother.

"Juan!" he said. "Juan's been bothering you again. What did he do? Tell me and I'll kill him."

Grace looked at him with a seriousness he had never seen before. "It's not Juan," she said quietly.

"Then what?"

"I just need to be alone right now. I need to think."

"About what?"

Grace turned to him. Her eyes said something he did not understand.

"What?" he whispered. What was happening to her?

"Ben," she began in a voice that was no longer a child's, "if I disappear one day, don't be worried. Don't look for me. There is something I need to do."

Ben looked into each of her eyes and nodded slowly. He knew he had to leave now. He didn't know what was going on or why. All sorts of thoughts raced through his head. Grace the witch. Grace the Great One. Grace the beautiful, magical young woman he loved. Who was she? Did Big M promote the desire to disappear? He thought about his father. Did he go through the same thing before he vanished? Did he hear some kind of calling, the same voice that now called Grace, his only love too?

He got up from the grass and brushed his knees.

"I'll bring my mother the flowers she needs," he said calmly, "You do what you have to do."

Grace rubbed the dirty clothes vigorously against the wash board in a bucket of cold water. She pictured the warm and welcoming face at the periphery of her mind, massive as the sky and more handsome than any man she ever imagined. She looked up at the serene Finger's Edge standing stoically on the horizon and wondered what secret it held for her.

The image haunted her all day long and invaded her sleep.

Peculiar dreams swallowed the night. Unlike the images that normally raided her sleep, these were deep and real. In one, she saw a giant finger rise from the dirt and beckon her to a place of eerie clouds alive with electricity. She refused the call, gathering blankets around her in a heap. Quickly, another dream followed. In this one, a great ghost of vapor enveloped her, like the steam from Din's stew. The white mist became thicker and thicker until she could no longer see. She awoke in a panic and gasping for air.

Dancing Wind opened her eyes. This was not the first time she was awakened by one of Grace's dreams. For years, she had felt the intense dreams through her own sleep, as if she had dreamed them herself. Since Grace never discussed them, Dancing Wind assumed they were the dreams that accompanied a young girl into womanhood. But this dream was different. She felt it gathering in her own throat too as she arose from her bed to comfort Grace. She stroked her hair gently, like she did when Grace was a little girl. Day was on the brink of night as light seeped through the window and through every crack in the old wood and mortar that constructed the Hogan. The new day made all objects visible.

"I'm all right, Din," she whispered.

"I will make you new dream catcher today." She took the net off the wall above Grace's head. The feathers were entangled and its web was broken.

"No, that's okay. I don't need a new one."

Dancing Wind's coal eyes found her, a trace of morning sun outlined her face. Grace quietly changed out of her nightclothes and into the long, red skirt she normally wore. She buttoned the yellow shirt up to her neck and left the top one open.

"Grace. I do not know what visions dance in your night, but I feel them. Your dreams hold a message."

Grace looked at Dancing Wind for a moment, then away.

"I know."

She took the bulging burlap bag resting by the door and quietly left the Hogan. A beam of light sifted into the room.

Grace felt the pink light warm her back and radiate across her shoulder blades. Her eyes fixed on Finger's Edge, towering in the new day. A faint mist hovered above it.

When she sprayed the seeds on the ground, the sound was strangely amplified in the morning silence. Chickens flapped their wings, chattered and hopped.

Grace couldn't take her eyes from Finger's Edge, glowing in the dawn's light. She stared at the small cloud hovering peacefully above it and hoped to see the face again.

Her thoughts were invaded by a strange sound. Low and incomprehensible, it sounded like a distant bell that chimed way in the back of her head. Then it grew louder, so loud that it encompassed everything. The ringing became a chant of voices, an indescribable blend of yearning, melodic sounds that formed no words. She tasted them and felt them sing all over her skin. The seed bag fell from her hands, enlisting a band of bouncing hens to gather in a feeding frenzy.

Grace was transfixed, her eyes glued to the horizon. She began to walk, in a trance, toward Finger's Edge.

~

Ben's night was disrupted by dreams as well. A terrible nightmare kept him awake much of the night. In his dream, he and Grace were about to marry. Grace wore a beautiful wedding dress made of silk and lace and her long dark hair danced freely under the soft white veil. The warm afternoon sun was suddenly eclipsed by a dark and sinister cloud. The wind became violent and odd. Instead of blowing, it sucked, plucking Grace out of the Earth. She screamed in fright as the wind inhaled her ferociously into infinity. A torn particle of the beautiful wedding dress drifted down from the sky. He looked up and saw her swimming in the air, her white gown turning black as she disappeared into a cloud like a witch.

He awoke in a sweat and stayed awake for hours before he could return to sleep. When he finally did, the pandemonium of gluttonous chickens shook him to his feet. He jumped into his pants and stepped outside.

Not even Dancing Wind knew exactly how long Grace was missing. Her only clue was an empty feeding bag amidst slobbering chickens and a few neighboring birds who were fatter than usual. She separated two squabbling hens with a stick then squinting at the silhouette of Finger's Edge that stood like a phantom in the distance. Sunlight soaked the cloud that hovered in a circle about the rock and spewed neon rays into the sky. A small smile disrupted the wrinkles on Dancing Wind's face. She knew Grace was up there somewhere. She touched the pouch at the end of her medicine necklace, stared at Finger's Edge and wondered what the reunion would bring.

Matilda looked at Ben with a growl he stormed half-naked out the door and toward the barn.

"Go see what's happening!" she ordered Maria.

Maria rolled her eyes and sighed. She brushed the trace of sleep from her eyelashes, wiped her hands and stepped out the door.

When Ben found Dancing Wind gazing at the looming red rock in the distance, he knew what happened. His feet slowed to a steady trot.

"Dancing Wind?" he whispered softly.

She moved her dark eyes towards him. He shook his head.

"No. She can't go there."

"Leave her be. She will return."

"I had a terrible dream. Something bad is going to happen to her. She can't climb that alone. It's dangerous!"

"Ben, when you were only five years old, you made the trip up Finger's Edge and back."

"No. I've got to get her! Something will happen if I don't."

He was already on his way, leaving only words in his wake.

~

Gnarled trees groped for the sky. Patches of green softened the ground. Vivid blue flowers grew between slabs of shimmering rocks. The sun beamed warmth on Grace's shoulders. She looked up and squinted at the large fiery ball. Walking through the untamed brush, she noticed the dirt was as soft as a sheepskin blanket.

The sky was clear and quiet and all that lodged in the vast blue above was a single, curious cloud. It was a puffy, fluffy wispy one, cute and small. There was an incredible peace here, soothing and warm, it radiated from her heart into all parts of her body. She sat down then fell back and stretched out on the soft dirt. Grace felt a rush. She was on top of the world looking straight up. Her feet tingled from the big climb and it felt good to rest them. She wiggled her toes and stared at the cloud above her.

It sat in the sky like a drop of buttermilk, churning slowly in a liquid blue, its movement barely detectable. Perhaps the cloud was breathing. Maybe it was alive. Grace let the silly thoughts consume her. She felt free with no chores and no Matilda. The grassy bed was like a giant cushion beneath her body and the fragrance from the violet petals perfumed the air. She breathed it all in and shut her eyes to savor the moment.

When she opened them again, the cloud was directly overhead. It moved like the flow of molasses, changing form ever so sluggishly and slowly transformed into a white bird whose wings stretched across the sky. Grace was amused. What else could this cloud be? Leisurely, it changed into another shape. The white wings bent in the subtle breeze to form what appeared to be two arms. Like vapor clay, this cloud molded a huge sombrero, just like Amando's. She laughed and wondered if the cloud would do whatever she wanted it to.

"Be a chicken!" she said. "Like the crazy hungry ones I left at the barn."

She stared at the sky and waited. The warm wind sculpted the cloud gently. Grace recognized the chubby white body, the stupid little head. There it was – a Big M chicken. She laughed out loud. What could she make it do next? Matilda?

She watched the cloud produce the shapes she desired, moving ever so slowly, barely notable by the human eye. It was like watching the movements of a clock's hands. *Time passes*, she thought, *but even if you watch the clock you can't see it*, just like this cloud whose imperceptible movements obeyed her every wish.

She watched its shape unravel like a bundle of cotton. While Grace was thinking, searching for another challenging shape, the cloud was forming something curious.

~

Matilda was furious when she learned her son swallowed the wake of the little witch to Finger's Edge.

"Dancing Wind!" she yelled. "Why didn't you stop him!"

Amando was at her side. Maria sat on a rock with her apron draped over her face to shield her from the smell of pigs.

"No harm." Dancing Wind was patient, considering she was rarely in the presence of the almighty Matilda.

"No harm! That little witch finally goes running back home to that devil's rock and my son goes with her!" Her voice shook the ground.

"Easy, Señora. Easy," Amando whispered to her gently, but Matilda never heard him. Juan found his way to the confusion and jumped off his horse. The chickens scattered, despite their lethargic state.

"I'll go get lover boy," he announced smugly, already hearing the situation from Matilda's booming voice.

"You stay out of this, Juan," said Amando. "And take your hat off!"

Juan rolled his eyes and smirked, leaving his sombrero just where it was.

"You wait," Amando threatened, shaking a finger at his son.

"I don't care who goes. One of you better go and get my son from that witch's nest!" she charged.

Dancing Wind shook her head slowly and rested her eyes upon the looming red finger on the horizon. She saw something too, hovering above Finger's Edge and her heart beat faster. She didn't see a cloud formation like this since the day Grace was found.

~

The cloud shaped itself into an oval as its airy mist moved with agility. Side by side, within the oval, appeared two holes. Grace watched quietly. Something was deliberately being formed.

Shades of gray appeared within the white form, creating the illusion of a face. Grace sat up nervously, keeping her gaze chained to the cloud above. She could see it now. Eyes emerged from the shadows of the gray-blue puffs and grew sharper. They were human eyes, the color of the sky. They were *her* eyes and they looked directly at Grace.

Fright wiped away any trace of amusement. These eyes were not a figment of her imagination. They were real, very real. Her forehead became hot with both excitement and fear while a chill went directly into her bones. It was the face of a man, the same man she saw before.

The cloud parted like cotton in the easy breeze. The face disappeared as the cloud resumed its identity as an innocent blob stretching across the sky.

"Grace!"

She jumped to her feet when she heard her name and searched the land and sky.

"Grace!"

Ben swam his way through the lanky brush the way he did as a child. But now his legs were long and strong, able to leap over the bog and rocks with ease. He saw Grace in the distance and ran to her.

"Grace!" he said with relief as his arms flew around her in a warm embrace. Grace was uncomfortable with his unabashed affection.

"I was so worried!" he spoke into her hair. She said nothing to him. This was her secret, one she would never share. He looked at the sky and took a deep breath. Grace saw him eye the cloud.

"I've forgotten how beautiful it is up here and how strange the clouds are."

Grace looked up and saw the cloud was now a thin shroud, singed by a late afternoon sun. Ben released his grip and stood still, soaking in the breeze with one breath. A gush of memories hit him. He remembered the feeling of a presence and a voice in the wind. He recalled the strange feeling of being watched and took Grace's hand. He did not care to feel that haunting sensation again.

"Grace, it's getting late. Let's go."

Grace brushed the dirt off her clothes and they started their decline. Once in a while she scanned the sky secretly and saw several orange cloud streaks invading the blue. Her cloud was gone, but the vivid eyes still lingered in her head.

Grace was eager to visit again. Though it was eerie and frightening, the experience felt strangely fulfilling. There was a sense that something was quenched inside of her, as if her heart was restored to its proper place and the bird that flew away with her spirit had finally returned.

She held fast to Ben's hand and descended into the valley.

CHAPTER SIX

Word of ten-pound lettuce heads, thirty-inch corncobs, pumpkin-sized potatoes, fifty-pound chickens, triple-yoked eggs and extra lean cattle found their way to ears everywhere. Orders and requests were flooding in from all over. A wire from as far away as Carson City and Tucson begged to purchase some of the now famous products from Big M.

Matilda blew out part of a laugh. The sound fell from her lips as she read the wire. Something jumped inside her, something she didn't quite recognize. It was joy, the kind she hadn't felt since Elmo proposed to her on that sawdust floor at Casa Grande years ago. Her face flushed. Maria stared and wiped her hands on the apron.

"Ben!" she roared out. "Ben!" Her voice found its way under the closed door of Ben's room. He shut his book and was forced to answer.

If he did not, he feared the shrilling scream would persist and break his eardrums.

"What?" He loafed down the stairs.

"Put a nice shirt on. You're coming with me!"

"Where?"

"Just shut up and do as I say. It's about time you learn something around here, boy."

"I have a right to know where we're going."

Matilda's nostrils flared. Ben retorted with a similar performance. Maria watched the noses compete.

"Must you always fight your mother?" She threw him the letter.

His eyes gobbled the words and looked to Matilda with surprise.

"I want you to come with me." She snatched the paper from his fingers. "Now hurry up. Dress!" She turned to Maria. "You will have to go into town to do the usual bidding. Amando is too busy today."

"Pero, Senora! No sabe bidding. I am just a servant!"

"You do as I say! I am the boss around here!" she exploded. "Tell Ben I will be waiting for him in the wagon." She stepped out and let the heavy oak door slam behind her.

~

Grace filled one more basket of giant green leaves, flicking a small bug from the edge. She looked up and saw a figure wobbling in the distance. As Maria waddled closer she held an apron to her nose in one hand and guarded her bouncing bosom with the other. *New orders from the queen*, she thought and braced herself. She already had plenty to do.

"Grace!" she heard Maria's voice totter. She slowed her pace as she approached Grace. Her breath was heavy.

"¡Grace, necesidad un favor!"

Grace brushed the soil from her hands and rose from the dirt. "Nobody is here. You must go to town por delivery. I cannot go. You go."

"Are you sure Matilda wants me to go into town?" she asked, a bit confused. Matilda went to great lengths to keep her out of sight. Why would she want her to go into town?

Maria nodded her head violently. "Si! Si! Take the wagon, fill up and go!" Maria raised the apron to her nose again, "Just go."

Without further words, she departed, waddling back to the big house on the horizon.

Grace looked around. Where would she start? She was never in town before. She didn't know the people there, who to speak to or what to sell. She told Dancing Wind who told her what she knew from years of tending to Big M. She thought nothing of this odd request. Matilda was unpredictable and capable of anything. To Dancing Wind, it was merely another chore to add to Grace's list.

Juan stopped brushing the horse when he saw Grace enter the stable. A devious smirk stretched across his face. He watched her hastily harness a horse to a wagon. She pretended not to see him as she quickly buckled the leather straps of a horse.

"Pretty little witch, aren't you?" The voice slid from his throat as he moved closer. Instantly, he was upon her and swiftly pinned her to the wall. She froze and glared at him. Juan's fingers combed through her smooth hair. "Mmm." He closed his eyes.

"Stop it!" she yelled, pushing his hands from her hair. His eyes flew open.

"You afraid of me?" The corners of his mouth curled up as he pressed his body against hers. "All witches are afraid of Juan."

A fury gathered up inside her. She pushed him away with an incredible force that surprised them both.

"Get away from me!"

Faster than the stunned Juan could see, Grace dashed to the wagon, jumped into the seat and snapped the reins. The horse bolted out of the barn, nearly stomping Juan with its gallop. He jumped out of the way and rolled on the ground.

Grace and Dancing Wind filled the wagon. They piled together bundles of gargantuan vegetables, extra large eggs (which were carefully packed in a carton of hay) and two canteens of water. The ride was long, hot and dry. Dancing Wind helped her prepare for the trip, telling her to follow the southern horizon until she came upon the town there. Grace stepped into the wagon seat with a sigh. She gave Dancing Wind one last goodbye before she embarked. Dancing Wind returned her hesitant gaze with a reassuring smile. Off Grace went, leaving Dancing Wind to watch her until she disappeared into the miles.

Alone for two hours, her thoughts drifted to Finger's Edge. She saw it protruding proudly from the horizon. A cool wind fanned her face. She removed her hat and allowed her hair dance in it. She was grateful of the sound of the horse's hooves, which prevented her mind from bursting in the vast, dead silence.

The wind blew, and in it she heard the voices again, yearning voices sang one long flat note. They called her name in hushed tones. She listened without fear, wondering if she really heard it or if her mind was playing tricks with the thundering silence. The large wooden wheels squeaked on the dry terrain. Grace's eyes soared to the sky. The stark canopy bore a single cloud, crisp and light. It accompanied her on the journey and did not take shape or form eyes, even through her mind dared it to. It was just a cloud. Maybe it was one of the Cloud People Dancing Wind told her about, or just a figment of her wild imagination.

When she arrived at town, all heads turned. Grace's crystal blue eyes, sun kissed face and flowing and rich hair took the breath away from both men and women alike. Merchants flocked at the sight of the wagon overflowing with the heartiest items they ever saw. They flocked too, around Grace. Her smile absorbed all who gathered around to bid top dollar for the wagon's wealth.

From then on, merchants in the town of Cottonwood demanded that Grace accompany each delivery.

It didn't take long before a few potential suitors to find their way to Big M in search of Grace. But before they could come anywhere near her, Matilda pulled out her double-barreled rifle and made certain they never showed their face again. For the first time, Ben approved of his mother's actions.

"Scoundrels," he called them. "Nobody's going to touch her."

When Matilda heard that, she knew for sure, Ben could not be trusted alone with Grace. She did not like the growing romance between the two. And now, because of popular demand, (which also resulted in better prices) when it came time to visit Cottonwood again, Matilda had to bring Grace.

"Curse that Maria!" she mumbled.

Maria was fired immediately after the incident. Matilda could not stand for such rebellious behavior. Now she was forced to deal with the little witch whenever she needed to do business in Cottonwood.

It was an uncomfortable event for both of them. As Matilda weighed the driver's side down, the wagon squealed in protest. Grace sat quietly. Matilda slammed a heavy bag beside her, which became a makeshift partition between herself and the witch. She snapped the reigns and the packed wagon groaned, inching its way up to a steady speed. Grace leaned back in an attempt to make herself comfortable. Matilda dared not look at her. She kept her eyebrows close to her eyes. Grace took a deep breath and forced a smile.

"Nice day."

The wagon bounced on the rugged terrain. The horse's shoes clopped against some rocks. The shriek of random birds cut through the quiet. Not a word came from Matilda. She just sat there, looking straight ahead, pretending no one was beside her. Grace sighed and accepted the fact she was riding with nothing more than an oversized stone.

She watched Finger's Edge as it moved across the horizon with the horse's speed and disappeared behind her. She leaned back, closed her eyes and took a deep breath in the warm desert sun. When she opened them, it was there again—that cloud.

She sat up, alert as she watched it dart across the sky with incredible speed. She never saw a cloud move that fast. It zoomed by the other clouds as it curled its body in circular motions until it was directly overhead. Grace was too engrossed in the phenomena to notice Matilda, who noticed her. She looked up, saw nothing unusual and gave Grace a suspicious glance.

The white puffy cloud immediately swelled with color– a charcoal green – *strange color for a cloud*, she thought. The cloud spread its body, like a cat seeking a nap, and plopped itself on the sun. The wind gained momentum, the sweet breeze became bitter. Matilda looked at the sky and saw the culprit, then looked at Grace, still looking skyward.

"What are you looking at!?" she blasted at Grace as the wind pulled strands of hair from her tightly wound bun. "Tell me!"

This direct communication took Grace's attention away from the sky. This was the first time Matilda addressed her in any way. Her eyes met Matilda's and she simply answered, "That cloud."

As Matilda raised her eyes to the cloud, it was as if the heavens spat on her face. A sudden downpour of rain fell violently. Matilda yanked the horse to a halt and blinked frequently as the drops fell off her brow and into her eyes. She shot a glance at Grace. Her eyes widened. Grace was dry! The land around her was dry! The dark cloud was only over Matilda's head. Grace couldn't help the urge that intoxicated her like wine. She cupped her mouth but the laughter spilled through her fingers anyway.

Matilda jumped off the wagon seeking to avoid the freak storm, but it followed her. Matilda crossed herself frantically uttering words in a language Grace did not understand.

"¡Santa Madre de Dios!" Matilda hopped in circles, as if trying to free herself from the storm with a shake. She stopped suddenly and looked at Grace who was laughing!

"Get off this wagon and WALK!" She erupted with a pointing finger.

Walk? They were miles away from home and miles from town. Matilda obviously didn't care. The water didn't extinguish the fire of Matilda's rage.

"If you can walk ALL THE WAY up that wretched mountain and ALL THE WAY BACK, you can WALK ALL THE WAY HOME!" Matilda's hair was drenched and stuck to her face. Her nose became a waterway. Grace quietly stepped off the wagon. Matilda jumped back on, dripping wet, snapped the reins with a holler and flew away. The dark cloud insisted on following her. Grace watched helplessly as the sound of the wagon and horses fell into silence. *Now what?* She thought to herself and looked up at the blank blue slate above.

After a mile, her feet began to hurt and the hot sun drew droplets of sweat from her skin. Her mouth was drier than the sand beneath her feet. She took off her hat, licked her dry lips and looked up. There it was again.

"Stupid cloud!"

Why did she laugh? It was the first time Matilda attempted conversation. Finally there was communication and that stupid cloud had to go and ruin it. She took off her shoes.

"Stupid!" she screamed again. "Look what you caused!"

The cloud hovered innocently, white and puffy, void of rain. It abandoned Matilda to bother her. Grace knew the cloud well. It was the one that haunted her on top of Finger's Edge and the one who foiled her sleep. It was following her. If anyone else saw her cloud, they wouldn't be able to separate it from the others. But she recognized this cloud, there was an odd familiarity about it. She kept walking and tried to ignore it, but the cloud pursued her.

"Get out of here!" she screamed to the sky. Her voice echoed off the distant canyons. "Go away! Stop bothering me!" She wiped the perspiration from her forehead. Her lips were cracked and brittle. She picked up the nearest rock and hurled it straight into the air, aiming to injure the celestial puff lurking above. She watched the rock disappeared into the blue horizon.

A sudden gust knocked her down and with it, came a rush of cool air. She heard it again.

"Grrrraaaaaaccccccccceeeeeee."

Now she was spooked. *This is really crazy*, she thought, a cloud with a face? A wind that spoke? What was happening to her? She was convinced she was going mad and the heat fried her brains. She stumbled to her feet and ran in a desperate attempt to escape the hovering cloud and the chilling voice.

"Stop!" She heard the voice say. It was a quick whisper inside her head, at the same time, all around her. She continued to run frantically, scared, covering her ears. A high-pitched ring began in the back of her head and got louder. Tiny dots danced before her eyes and her knees buckled.

"Grraaacceeee," a hushed voice sang out as she dropped to the ground, weakened by heat exhaustion.

It started to rain, gently and softly. Drops of water fell directly into Grace's mouth, quenching, refreshing and reviving her with cool liquid. She sat up and felt no more fear. Instead, she felt consumed with life and inflated with joy. She brushed the damp hair away from her face. The shower was sufficient enough to restore her and brief enough not to drench her. She got to her feet and swallowed a long, luxurious breath of sweet desert air. She touched her mouth. Her lips were moist and there was no sign of the sun's bite.

She found a strange and new comfort in the cloud that followed her home. Grace returned to Big M with barely a limp in her walk.

CHAPTER SEVEN

Fear forced Matilda into a decision. In the short time it took her to leave her house and walk to the Hogan, Matilda convinced herself that her luck really did change and it wasn't because of Grace. She needed to rid herself of the witch once and for all. *She* was the boss and nobody was going to tell *her* what to do and who she should have on her land. Grace proved herself to be a witch that afternoon and Matilda believed her to be a danger to both she and her son.

She lived in the shadow of this little witch for too long, who now seemed to be a possessed devil. She gave Grace too many chances. She had to take care of the matter before things got worse, before it was too late for Ben. She had to protect her son, no matter what.

Matilda burst into the Hogan and monopolized the doorway. Her sudden presence startled Dancing Wind and Grace. Her wrinkled brow created a wicked crease in her forehead as she loosed her necklace and held a silver crucifix at Grace's face, fully expecting her to shrink in its presence.

"WITCH!" she yelled. "Devil witch! Today, you proved it!"

Grace sought safety in Dancing Wind's arms.

"That wasn't me," she said calmly. "I didn't do that."

Matilda continued to hold the cross at Grace, moving closer to her. Dancing Wind held Grace tighter.

"Grace told me what happened," she whispered in her textured voice, "and she was as scared as you were."

"No she wasn't! She enjoyed it. She laughed at me!"

Grace shook her head. Matilda's eyes were red with anger.

"Do you know what they do to witches here?" Spit flew from Matilda's mouth as the words rushed out.

Grace shook her head. For the first time, Matilda frightened her. Of all the strange things that happened that day, Matilda had to go and lose the rest of her mind too. Dancing Wind held Grace tighter as Matilda lurked cautiously closer, she knew what they did to witches. She heard many stories of shootings, whippings, hangings, floggings, stoning. These were the ways they executed witches in this superstitious region. Not just witches but Indians too.

"Don't worry. I'm not going to kill you." Matilda's voice sounded maniacally drunk. "That's what they do to witches around here, you know. That's what they do." She showed her teeth in strange delight. "But that's not what I'm going to do with you."

Grace listened.

"I'm going to give you a chance to flee. Be free, witch, be free!" she closed her eyes, in a chant.

Dancing Wind and Grace looked at each other. Matilda had gone mad. Her eyes flew open.

"But one thing I ask in return, that you remove the spell from my family. That you spare the life of my son."

Grace didn't know what to say and neither did Dancing Wind.

"Say yes! Say yes!" she yelled.

Ben heard the commotion and arrived at the Hogan.

"Ma! What's going on? What are you doing with that cross?"

"She's a witch, Ben. She proved it today."

Ben tried to pry the silver medallion away from her grip, but Matilda's elbow kept him away.

His eyes remained on Grace and his heart burned with love for her. She was going to be his wife one day and he had to protect her.

"Mother!" Ben raised his voice. Matilda jerked her head towards him.

"Shut up." She turned quickly towards Grace again. "Make me a promise!" she demanded.

"NO!" shouted Grace in a voice no one ever heard pass through her lips before.

Ben's mouth fell open.

"NO! I am NOT a witch!" Grace protested in a rage that made her face flush. She stood up, walked towards Matilda and their eyes locked. Matilda took two steps back, her true fear exposed.

"I am not a witch and I don't have to take this from you anymore! If there is any witch around here, it is you!"

Matilda's eyes widened with Grace's defiant words. She hurled the ornate cross at Grace, which struck her in the forehead and caused her to bleed. Dancing Wind gasped.

"Matilda!" was all she could say.

Ben ran to Grace. She ignored him as her angry eyes focused on Matilda who held her breath in anticipation for the worst.

"I am not a witch," she whispered as the blood oozed from her wound, "and I refuse to be your slave anymore." She wiped the blood, looked to Dancing Wind and told her with her eyes that everything would be fine. She walked past the silenced Matilda, a stunned Ben and out the door.

Ben could not take it any longer, he couldn't watch Grace leave. He loved her so much. He turned to his mother with rage.

"You're a crazy, horrible, stupid woman and I don't care if you're my mother. I never want to see you again!" He stormed away. Dancing Wind glared at Matilda, who pretended not to notice and vanished from the doorway.

Grace gazed up at Finger's Edge as dusk settled upon the ranch. She saw her cloud in the distance. He waited for her.

"Grace, please don't leave." Ben's voice quivered as he ran after her. His eyes were filled with tears he did not conceal. "Please. We need you here. Dancing Wind needs you. I need you. Please, don't listen to my mother, she's just a crazy, superstitious woman. Stay here. Please." Ben quickly wiped away the tear that managed to escape his eye. Grace looked at him with sadness.

"I have to leave. I can't take the blame any more."

"You can't leave," Ben sniffled. "Imagine what will happen to us, to me."

With all his schooling, he just could not comprehend the simple thing Grace tried to tell him. She looked into his brown eyes and saw a little boy.

"Ben, you're my friend, and this is not the end. It's just a small break. No one knows what the future holds."

"Grace," he said with a laugh, "Grace, I've got an idea! Let's you and me get married and run away from here."

Grace's smile faded and her eyebrows curled in confusion. "Marry?"

"Well, we can elope! We don't need that big wedding thing!"

"Ben," she said softly, "Ben, I can't marry you."

The joy drained from his smile. "What do you mean? Why?"

She took a deep breath. "Please understand. I love you but we can't marry."

"What? Is it another man?"

Grace shook her head. Poor Ben refused to understand.

"No Ben, I just have to go." She paused and looked at him. He was silent, drinking up the violet reflections in her crystal eyes.

"Ben," she began gently, "don't come after me. If you love me, do this for me. Please. Promise me this."

He was mesmerized by her sparkling gaze and reluctantly nodded to her request.

"Oh, muchacho, you make me want to throw up," Juan interrupted the tender moment with his gritty laugh. He had been watching for some time, plucking petals off a flower as he quietly inched his way closer to them.

Ben swung around with sudden fury and with one swift blow, sent Juan to the ground. Grace was frightened by Ben's explosive rage.

Juan held his sore cheek and slowly got up, giving Ben a sinister glare.

"You wait muchacho...you wait. I will get you."

The two locked eyes for one powerful moment as Juan brushed the dirt from his pants and stood up. With one last threatening look, he walked away.

~

Grace packed a simple bag. There wasn't much she needed except for a change of clothes, a pot and a blanket. She kissed Dancing Wind gently on the forehead.

"Din, I will be back. I must do this."

Dancing Wind nodded slowly. A tear emerged from her coal eye and trailed over the dry terrain of her face, for the first time in decades. Grace fought back her own tears.

"Din, I will be back. Don't cry. I love you."

Dancing Wind sat quietly, eating up the last morsels of Grace's presence. She removed her cherished necklace and placed it over Grace's head.

"This will guide you and give you strength. Wear it always."

"But Din, this is yours."

Dancing Wind shook her head and wiped away the tears that eroded her desert skin.

"You will need it more than me. I am old. You carry on for me."

"Din, don't talk that way. You will live forever. You need to be here for me, to guide and raise me."

"I cannot live forever, my Grace. Take my medicine pouch and let Great Spirit guide you."

Grace burned an indelible image of Dancing Wind's into her memory.

"I'll be back, Din. I'll see you very soon. I promise. Please take care of the chickens for me. Make sure the cows get a kiss every morning and see that only gentle words are spoken to the vegetables."

Dancing Wind smiled and nodded. "Remember Grace, life is a circle. There is an end, there is also a beginning. Remember that, my dear little Grace."

Grace nodded and took the words to heart. She kissed Dancing Wind again and left the Hogan without another word. Dancing Wind's eyes remained on Grace long after she was gone.

Finger's Edge was her home, her land and her history.

The climb was remarkably simple and tireless. The top was as breathtaking as she remembered. She was wiser and more confident than she was the first time she visited. She walked through the brush and rugged terrain to the clearing and now she realized this space was meant for her, a home prepared by some unknown ancestor. She was eager to find out who tended to the land and abandoned her here seventeen years ago. She put the bag down and sat on the cushioning soil. The sun felt warm against her bare shoulders. She could dress anyway she pleased up here and there was no one to tell her what to do or where to go or what to say. This was her private place, her home.

She reclined and stretched out. She felt so alive and smiled at the hearty cloud gliding overhead.

"Who are you?" she asked. There was no response. Grace laughed.

"You're just a cloud, that's all!" she laughed. "I can't believe I'm expecting you to talk to me. What's the matter with me?"

She shut her eyes and basked in the rays. Her mind drifted in abstract thoughts as sleep beckoned her to concede. But something made her eyes pop open. She was not alone.

Grace stared at the cloud directly overhead, but it was not a cloud anymore, but a handsome face, the same face she saw once before. Could this be the same cloud that tormented her in the desert? His face was kind and gentle and he her so adoringly, it took her fear away. She was soothed by his presence and became aware of her heart beating profusely. Yes, her heart was very much there.

"Who are you?" she asked again.

The celestial being did not move his mouth to speak, but continued to gaze at her, blinking dreamily. She forgot this was a cloud, just a mass of white vapor. He *was* human. She wanted to reach out and touch him, touch his billowing hair, his soft lips. He was a ghost. Or, was he a dream? Did she drift off, unaware she was really asleep? The wind whispered in her ear with the same voice she heard before, the voice in her head, the voice in the desert, the voice of the cloud. It answered her question with one unusual sound.

"Ooooovvvvv."

"Ov?" Did she heard right or was it just the sound of her imagination?

"OV!" she shouted out loud and the cloud beamed. "*That's* your name." She repeated the word like a chant and it rose from her throat like the air she exhaled.

The smiling face melted into vapor and slowly resumed the shape of a cloud. Still she wondered if she was merely dreaming.

"Come back," she said in a voice only she could hear. "Please."

The face was gone. Grace wondered why he disguised himself as the small cloud moving languidly across the sky. As other clouds meandered through, she wondered if they had faces too, although none of them seemed as familiar as her cloud Ov.

Everyday she saw the face and began to accept it. She wasn't crazy. She wasn't dreaming. Ov was real and became her new friend in the cool silence of Finger's Edge. Grace had long talks, mostly monologues with Ov. She told him all about Big M and Matilda, Din and Ben. She told him how Ben found her on Finger's Edge and why she returned. The face loomed and listened.

"I felt something missing before, but not anymore. Not when I'm here, not when I'm with you," she professed to the sky. "This is where I belong."

Grace cultivated a small harvest with the wild berries and greens she discovered growing bountifully among the blue flowers. She grew vegetables and fruits as nature willingly obeyed her simple desires. She had enough to keep her nourished and satisfied. Grace made a small dwelling for herself in a rock cavity near the clearing. When it rained, she collected water in the pot she brought. With the help of Ov, she eventually discovered a small spring well hidden in between rocks and a thick brush. He spoke directly to her thoughts like the voice of intuition and she sometimes responded with her mind.

Time went by. Grace was happy living on Finger's Edge.

When it got too quiet, when she yearned for company, when Ov was not there, the wind sang to her. She hummed the melodic ballads the wind taught her. She felt content and satisfied with life.

Grace was finally home.

~

Matilda wiped the sweat from her forehead. The hot sun beamed down in waves of steam. In the haze she saw Amando shimmering in the distance. She rolled up her sleeves. Giant stains from her armpits extended to her back as she walked towards him. Amando shook his head and removed his hat.

"Señora, there is not one left." He made the sign of the cross then looked to the sky. "Señora, not for thirteen weeks has it rained. They died of thirst."

"Why didn't you bring them to the water, you fool!" Sweat poured from her face like rain.

Amando shook his head. "They would not go."

"What are you talking about? This is nonsense!"

"Señora, they would not go. Like everything else here."

Matilda looked at him as his face glistened in the heat.

In the thirteen weeks since Grace was gone, the vegetables refused to grow. The chickens held in their eggs. The cows' udders dried up and now this. All the lean cattle that made Big M famous were now dead.

"There are maybe two left. Or three," said Amando, fanning his face with his sombrero. "Señora, I hate to tell you, but...."

"Then don't tell me, I don't want to hear it."

A serious draught plagued Big M for that span of time. The well was dry, so Matilda sent hands into town to fetch water. Matilda had problems in towns and villages everywhere. She was no longer welcome anywhere because of her rude and cavalier behavior when the ranch was in demand. In thirteen weeks, Big M went from a profitable, promising, productive ranch to a complete disaster. Word spread quickly and no one wanted anything to do with Big M. Even her neighbor Kilbee was doing far better and was gaining fast popularity in all the places Matilda once had.

Ben was long gone. He moved to Prescott City and attended school. Matilda sent men there to fetch him. Big M was sinking and she needed his help.

Amando caught her staring at Finger's Edge. Matilda's gaze was hard. He read the words that spilled from her eyes.

"Señora, you mustn't think that way." He lit the cigarette that dangled from his lips. Matilda broke her thought and gazed at him. She said nothing.

"You know what you must do," he said calmly, as smoke rose from his lips. "They say that those who are born without a guardian angel, such as yourself, must do other things in their lives to insure protection."

"Like what?" She wiped the sweat droplets that gathered under her nose. Amando took a long drag and let the smoke billow out in steaming curls.

"You do not want to hear this, Señora."

"Tell me, Amando." She leaned closer, "Do you have another recipe for me?"

Amando stared at Finger's Edge, then at Matilda. He removed the smoldering cigarette from his mouth.

"First, you must face the sun and stare into it. While you do this, you must ask for protection three times, then close your eyes and spit into the air three times. Then, you must...I don't know, Señora. I don't know if you want to hear this."

"Tell me. Please, Amando. I am in need," she said in the smallest voice Amando ever heard pass through her lips.

"Well, okay. I will tell you. You must then go and retrieve the bruja."

"NO!" She crossed her arms across her bosom. "This is a trick! I will not bring that witch back! I will not, Amando! I had enough!"

Amando shrugged his shoulders and raised his eyebrows. He took another puff.

"Well, what can I say? This is what you must do. Those who are under a spell, without protection, must surrender to certain things. Your burden is that girl. Without her, your curse flourishes."

"No, I will not bring her back! There must be something else I can do!" She took his arm, and whispered, "I fear the witch."

Amando shook his head.

"No, Señora, I have nothing else to suggest."

Matilda glared at him, waved the lingering smoke from her nose and walked away.

~

"Please protect me. Please protect me. Please protect me."

Matilda squinted into the young sun that rose slowly into the sky. She spit three times at the sky. One of them landed in her eye. She wiped it and cursed.

Juan was in the stall brushing a horse when Matilda stormed in. "Juan. You must go to Finger's Edge and retrieve that little witch!"

Juan smugly looked at Matilda then boasted a big smile. He didn't have to think twice. "With pleasure, Señora."

Matilda raised her eyebrow at his sudden politeness.

~

Like every other morning, she arose to greet the giant face with a smile and embrace. The only way she could embrace Ov was to embrace the Earth. She stretched out, naked on the cushioning grass and gazed at Ov. She absorbed his affection and felt desire. Even though they saw each other and could communicate, it was not enough. A giant invisible wall divided them. She wished she could fly. She wanted to jump up and touch him but not even the highest mountain would was tall enough. This saddened her. Her heart wanted to leap out, but it was trapped in a mortal body. She dug her fingers into the dirt and closed her eyes, pretending it was Ov.

She became aware of a strange feeling. She opened her eyes and looked at Ov's face. Something was wrong. The folds of his face wrinkled in pain. Or was it in fear? She felt a teardrop on her skin and touched the medicine pouch on her necklace.

"What's the matter?" she whispered, hugging the ground tighter. She heard the voice again. It said something she wasn't sure it said. The wind spoke again,

"Go."

She sat up quickly. There was trouble at Big M.

Grace looked at Ov. He vanished into a vapor. Just then, she heard the rustling of bushes. She felt someone was watching her and looked around but saw nothing. She sought a sign in the sky. The faceless cloud stood still, watching in disguise. The wind said nothing.

Juan popped out from a wall of grass. Grace gasped as his eyes took in her naked body. He slithered towards her. Grace ran to cover herself, seized with fear and found her skirt. She wrapped herself with it as Juan approached with a sinister laugh. He moved slowly and took his time. He knew she was his. Grace grabbed a large, gnarled stick, but it didn't scare him.

"Come here, you little witch. Come here."

"Get away from me!" she shouted, waving the stick. Juan moved closer and forced the stick from her hand. He laughed again, moving his body closer to hers.

"Get away from me!" she screamed as he tore the skirt away and pulled her bare body towards him. Flushed with anger, fire rose from her belly and blew out as a scorching scream that sent birds out of trees and pebbles from canyons. Juan covered her mouth and trapped her with his arms.

"Ai! Where's your lover boy now?" Juan spit through manic laughter.

She struggled with Juan while in her mind she called for help. *OV! Help me! Please!*

At that moment, a sudden gust tore Juan away from Grace and threw him to the ground with tremendous force. Ov stretched across the sky and seized the sun. Troops of clouds joined him, swirling in a circle. The wind pinned Juan to the Earth. Grace got up and hastily covered herself. She watched Juan struggle, fighting the wind with gasps of breath. He looked at her with angry eyes and found the strength to stand. He walked against the ferocious blast towards her.

"I'm going to get you!" he gasping as he spoke.

The clouds swirled in the wind, creating a funnel, which sucked Juan off his feet and twisted him in the air. Juan screamed like a frightened boy. Grace, seized with terror, watched the panting man wrestled in vane to touch his feet to the ground. The wind carried Juan to the edge, then abruptly ceased. Juan dropped from the sky and plunged to the ground. Grace heard his scream echo in the canyons until it was gone.

"No!" she heard herself whisper in a clenched throat. She shut her eyes and covered her face. Grace witnessed the wrath of the heavens and it shocked her. She looked up and saw the clouds drifting away from each other. Trembling, she tried to look off the edge but couldn't see what fate demised the mischievous Juan.

Her hands quivered and her stomach ached. A sinking feeling

engulfed her heart. She had to go to Big M.

She was so shaken that it took her a whole day before she found the strength to climb down the side of Finger's Edge. She did not see Ov anywhere nearby, nor did she beckon him to appear. *This is murder*, she thought. *This is wrong.* She was now confused and afraid.

By the time she reached the base of Finger's Edge, the sky swelled with rain. Charcoal clouds were thicker than pillows. Lightening ignited the gray with blinding brightness. Grace felt her heart shrivel.

A crackle of thunder shook the ground as her feet flew to the Hogan. Veins of crooked light broke free of a cloud and ran its fingers along the horizon. Big, fat drops slapped the ground. Matilda opened the front door and stood out in the rain. A small smile managed to find her lips.

Amando opened the door of his bungalow and took his hat off, letting the driblets soak his hair. Rosa peeked out behind him. "Where's Juan?"

Grace opened the door of the Hogan and stopped. Water ran off her long dark hair and dripped down her back. She blinked her eyes. "Din?"

Grace could not tell if the water that poured down her face was from the sky or from her eyes. A chicken struggled and yelled, desperately trying to free itself from Dancing Wind's stiff hands.

"Din? I told you I'd be back. Din?"

Dancing Wind sat on a sheepskin rug and leaned against the wall in a lifeless stare to the ground. Grace moved to her and felt Dancing Wind's skin was cold.

Salty water rained from Grace's eyes as heavily as it fell from the clouds. She embraced Dancing Wind's body.

"Din. No, Din." She kissed the cold, dry skin. "I told you I'd be back soon. Why couldn't you wait?" She whispered though tears, "Why couldn't you wait for me?"

Grace wiped her eyes. "Din. You can't leave." She sniffled as she released the bird from Dancing Wind's stiff grip. The chicken hopped away with its feathers ruffled and missing.

"You lucky beast. You'll never know this sorrow." Grace closed

Dancing Wind's coal eyes forever. Quietly, she stepped outside.

"Ov!" she cried to the sky. "Why?"

There were so many clouds but she couldn't see him.

"Ov!" She scanned the thick, soupy sky.

"Guide Dancing Wind's spirit to the Great Place," she shouted to the sky with a quivering voice. Sorrow strangled her. If only she arrived sooner, when Dancing Wind was still alive.

"OV!" she cried, gushing with tears. "Ov!"

She saw him. His face emerged from the hundreds clouds that thickened the sky. She stared at his soothing, serene face and took solace.

As she gazed at him, he began to slowly transform. The folds of his misty face multiplied, his blue eyes darkened, becoming small and black. Grace instantly recognized what she saw. Warmth spread over her as the face beamed.

"Din!"

Dancing Wind's face was as big as the sky. Droplets of joy sprouted from her eyes. Din was all right. Grace stared at Dancing Wind until her face melted into the rest of the clouds. Grace knew Din was okay now. She was with Ov.

From the distance, Matilda watched Grace talk to the sky with intense emotion.

~

When Juan didn't come home, Amando and Rosa began to worry. They searched the land and asked the other ranch hands if they had seen their son.

"Señora Matilda, I must ask you, have you seen Juan?" Amando took his hat off. For the first time, she noticed his usually confident face strained with worry. "No one has seen him since yesterday."

"I sent him off to fetch the witch."

Amando's weary eyes widened. "You sent him up there?"

"Yes, Amando. Isn't that what you advised? To bring the witch back to Big M?"

"But you sent my son?"

"Yes, Amando! Who else would I send?"

Amando clenched his teeth and shook his head.

"You could have sent anybody else. You have plenty of ranch hands! Why did you send *my* son?" Amando was loud and angry.

Matilda's eyes narrowed. She never heard him speak in such a tone before.

"Amando! What's wrong with you? You yourself said that Juan was protected from any witch. What's wrong with you!"

"Juan is *my* son. *I* tell him what to do!"

"Juan *works* for me, you fool. I tell him what I please!"

Amando threw his hat on the floor. "You had better find my son!"

"Talk like that will get you fired!"

Amando picked up his hat and put it back on his head.

"You know Finger's Edge is a bad place. You know how I feel. Now my son is gone. Just like Elmo, my son is GONE!" He rushed out and let the heavy door slam behind.

Ben saw Amando storm from the house and brush by him without his usual friendly *Ai*. He watched Amando, walk in the direction of the Hogan and followed him there.

Grace sat alone under a tree. The rain finally ceased and the sky was clearing. Ben felt his heart hasten when he saw her. He returned to Big M at the request of his mother and secretly hoped to see Grace. She was back from Finger's Edge and he missed her so. Amando arrived there first. He knelt down next to her and tapped her arm.

"Juan. Where is he?"

Grace looked up at him and noticed a tremble in his voice. She shook her head slowly. "I don't know."

Amando looked at her. Ben neared.

"You must know where my son is. He came to fetch you!" Amando's voice grew cold. He grabbed Grace's arm and a tear fell from her eye.

"You must know!" His voice was soaked with desperation. Grace could shook her head. The memory of what happened on Finger's Edge was too much. She couldn't tell Amando what the wind did to his son. He would never believe her.

"Grace!" There was joy in Ben's voice as he approached her.

Amando looked up at him and got to his feet. Ben noticed the solemn look on his face. He saw Grace's eyes, heavy with sorrow.

"What's wrong? What's going on?" He was confused.

"Have you seen Juan?" Amando asked with piercing, suspicious eyes.

"No. Why?"

"He is missing," he said through clenched. "Don't you know anything?"

Ben saw the accusation in his dark, swollen eyes as Amando walked away. Ben looked to Grace and knelt beside her.

"What's wrong?"

Grace rubbed her eyes and shook her head.

"Did Amando hurt you?"

"No."

"Juan?"

She looked at him with red eyes.

"I'll kill him if he hurt a hair on your head!"

"Din is gone."

Ben was silent, his heart sank yet swelled at the same time. He put his arms around Grace and kissed her forehead, blinking away tears that blurred his vision. He looked towards the barn. A few chickens danced in front of the quiet, round Hogan, spraying feathers everywhere.

"Dancing Wind is gone…" he said in quiet disbelief.

~

The burial was small, attended only by Ben and Grace. Matilda didn't want to know anything about it. She was relieved the old woman was finally dead.

Ben and Grace silently buried Dancing Wind in the back of the Hogan next to the stump of a tree, which marked her grave with a simple epitaph that Ben inscribed with a knife. It read: *Here lies one who danced between Heaven and Earth.* Grace and Ben spoke little. The quiet between them grew large and dense as Ben began to feel Grace's heart floating farther and farther away from him. He felt sad and alone. Ben kissed her on the cheek and went home after the burial. Grace was too consumed with sadness to be aware of Ben's feelings.

Grace stepped inside the Hogan and looked around the empty room. She noticed the entangled, worn dream catcher with its web punctured. She noted Din's bed, which was just as she left it. The little jars containing the elements of life still remained where Dancing Wind first put them.

Her footsteps resonated on the bare earth floor, emphasizing the emptiness she felt. She knelt down by one of the jars, thick with dust, hay and feathers, blew off the residue and picked it up. In all the years she lived in the Hogan, she never touched these sacred jars. She yearned to open them. She tried to pry the cork of one free, but it was jammed. She thought perhaps she should leave it be. All these years the sacred jars preserved Dancing Wind's secrets and maybe were not meant to be opened. Grace placed the clay jar back where it was.

Dancing Wind's scent lingered. If she listened to the walls, she wondered if she could still hear Dancing Wind's tales of Finger's Edge. She wondered if every beam of wood, every blade of hay, every feather held Dancing Wind's words, thoughts and dreams. Grace wrapped a small, woven blanket around her and closed her eyes. Perhaps she could soak in the spirit Din worked into every weave.

She pictured Dancing Wind in the cloud that was Ov and wondered if the two met. It was so strange to see her face, Ov's face, *any* face in a cloud. Perhaps everyone saw what she saw and didn't discuss it, like an unspoken rule no one dared to break. What if everyone had a cloud person, their own private guide, the only cloud you can see and communicate with?

She heard stories from Ben, poems he read about mystical creatures with wings and glowing halos crowning their heads. These invisible beings flew around and watched over people all day long. She wondered if anyone ever really saw one of these angels. What if angels were really cloud people? There they are: cumulus, nimbus, cirrus, strata, the spirits of loved ones in the form of vaporous beings embracing the Earth like shapeless ghosts protecting us. *You could see them anytime you want*, she thought, even though they were in disguise all the time. When the sky was clear, they watched from afar. Sometimes they masqueraded as the morning dew or the mist that hovered above rivers and lakes. On a cold day, they appeared as our smoky breath. They lingered in the air around us, invisibly penetrating our souls with every breath we take. Who were they?

Was it strange to feel what she felt for a cloud? She snuggled the blanket around her and sighed so loud, she interrupted the singing crickets. Ov was so much more than a cloud, because in him was a piece of her – the other half of her heart. With his acquaintance came new vision. She now saw colors no other human could and felt the pulse of every being, every particle of life living and breathing.

She acknowledged the souls that lived in trees, in stars, in rocks and in all Mother Earth's creatures. Dancing Wind taught her that everything had a soul and we must treat all things with kindness and respect.

The lids of her eyes fell like a heavy curtain. Slumber kidnapped her thoughts until morning broke with an unusual commotion.

"Go!" the voice in her head demanded. "Leave!"

She stirred. The light that spilled into the small window was almost white, and Grace knew it was already mid-morning. Voices cut through the dense, hot air and awoke her.

Grace stepped on the dewy grass outside and saw Matilda talking with some ranch hands.

"Go!" Came the voice again. Grace looked up at the brilliant ball of sunlight that instantly warmed her hair. The sky was clear. She looked west and saw the Finger that summoned her home.

Grace looked to the vegetables, still brown and sickly, but noticed some bright green shoots at the base of their stems. She looked at the cows and the chickens and saw they were content.

She stepped inside the Hogan and wrapped all four jars in a blanket, tying the bundle securely with a fringed rope.

It was time to leave again.

~

It was draped over the back of a horse, its fingers fanned out like tree branches, its knees bent, exposing the worn soles of its boots. Kilbee and one of his ranch hands found the twisted, rigid body nearby.

"Matilda, I believe this is one of yours," Joseph said slowly. Matilda successfully disguised her shock with a stern brow and stiff lip. She inspected the corpse and knew instantly, even before she drew close enough to inhale the foul odor, it was Juan.

"This is one of mine." She stepped away from the decaying flesh. "Where did you find it?"

Kilbee pointed at Finger's Edge.

She shook her head. How was she going to tell Amando? Kilbee and his ranch hand dismounted and began to lift the body off the horse.

"Where would you like him?" Kilbee said in his usual polite manner.

"On that horse," she said and pointed in the direction of Amando's home. "Bring him over there. That's where the boy's father is."

Kilbee mounted his horse again and looked at Matilda, whose face showed no sign of remorse.

"It's that witch, you know," she said with a frown. "Should've let you have her long ago."

"Maybe you should've."

He shook his head in disappointment and brushed the smell of death from his hands. Matilda pretended not to hear.

Kilbee slowly rode down the hill, holding the reins of the horse that carried Juan's remains. Matilda watched them trot down the hill and took a deep breath.

She saw Amando open the door and watched him fall to the ground in dismay. The men hoisted the stiff body off the horse. Matilda blinked away the unusual trace of liquid that intruded upon her vision. For a moment, she imagined she was Amando and Juan was her son and felt the squeezing, clenching pain he felt in his heart. But that moment of true empathy was quickly stolen by the sound of invading footsteps.

"What is going on?" Ben came out, buttoning his dress shirt and looked. He saw the men carry a body into the small bungalow. Matilda composed herself, thankful that Ben was alive and well.

"Who is that?"

"Juan." The word fell bluntly from Matilda's mouth.

"He's dead?" Ben was bewildered. "How?"

"Grace killed him."

She turned away from the view and stepped into the house. Ben remained and watched as Amando rose to his feet. The Mexican looked his way for one powerful moment. Ben felt Amando's dark eyes pierce him with anger, sorrow and revenge. His fiery eyes forced Ben back into the house.

~

Amando slid lead down the shoot of his double-barreled rifle. The sombrero's shadow masked his hot face and blood-shot, bitter eyes. Streams of smoke spewed from his nose. A dirty, sweat-soaked cigarette dangled from his chapped lips.

Rosa sat still, staring out the window with a plain linen handkerchief attached to her nose. Her large body hid the seat of the small raw chair that groaned occasionally in the dark and dingy home. Amando coughed. Rosa remained, unmoved by any sound, her face dampened by tears. She did not shift her eyes to see her husband. It had been four days since they buried their only son and now, Amando was ready.

"No one kills my Juan," he mumbled with a phlegm infested throat and wiped his eyes. He tossed the loaded weapon over his shoulder and stepped out the door.

A flock of riders gathered, ranch hands mostly and a few personal friends of Amando came from neighboring ranches to join the posse. Amando climbed on his horse and led the pack towards the monolith rock that appeared in his eyes, as the devil's wicked horn.

A trail of thick smoke billowed from horse's hooves as they charged towards the looming rock.

Matilda watched the ensuing clouds rise from the band of galloping horses. She watched alone. Ben already left the ranch and headed back to the city. When he saw Grace was gone, he respected her wishes and did not try to find her. He felt lost, confused and sad. There was nothing left at Big M for him. He found no reason to stay home at Big M and live with his mother. Ben had no idea of the events that ensued at the ranch after he left and Matilda didn't make an effort to inform him.

Matilda watched the horizon and thought of her son. Her eyes followed the moving mob and willed them to find the witch and get rid of her once and for all.

~

Grace did not hear the angry group gathered at the base of her home. She did not hear their frustrated cries as they attempted again and again to ascend the steep rock in vain. She did not hear Amando empty his rifle with sounding pops that echoed in the canyons. Grace couldn't possibly know the futile rage and confusion that collected like knotty waters at the foot of Finger's Edge. She could not know any of this, for she was completely submerged in the vision she beheld.

Hot tears fell from her eyes. She cried for Juan. She cried for Amando, for Dancing Wind and for Ov. It didn't matter what Ov did to Juan, she thought, because Ov saved her from the danger Juan intended. Ov was her protector. She loved him so much and knew he saved her life. Grace stared into his eyes and felt a sensation that was real.

He kissed her.

Grace touched her lips and felt a trace of mist. It was odd. She did not see him bend down to kiss her, though her eyes were on him all the time. But still, she felt it. With an unblinking stare, she gazed at the heavenly face. Ov was no longer the ghost-like apparition she was so used to seeing. Grace saw a face that was real and human, made of flesh. He blinked slowly as his brows curled in sorrowful compassion. She wished he could comfort her. She wished he could touch her skin and hold her. She wanted him to wipe her tears away, but Ov was so far away. She closed her eyes and imagined him human and whole, his strong young body wrapped around hers. She felt every part of him as they melted together in a swoon of passion. She sighed in sorrow and opened her eyes. Imagination was no substitute for the real thing. She looked at the face hovering above hers and longed for him.

She imagined what she looked like to him – so small, so distant, on the grassy surface. Could they be together one day? Was there enough time to spend with each other if they could be united? Was time an illusion to a cloud? Maybe there was no such thing as time to the Cloud People. Maybe the only gauge of time for clouds were the humans they watched grow old and die. Grace wondered if Ov would watch her wither through time and grow old and wrinkled like Din. If only she was a cloud, she could live forever with him in timeless love.

Grace wondered if anyone ever loved a cloud the way she did. Sometimes she even wondered if Ov was really the love of someone else. Did everyone have a cloud of their own, or was this a unique situation? Did other clouds know about their affair? Did they even care? Grace dared to think about Matilda. Did she have a cloud too? Maybe one of them was hers – a dark cloud, like the one that lingered over her head in the desert. She laughed to herself and wondered if anything watched over Matilda at all.

As Grace's eyes delighted in the sky, she imagined a time before history was ever recorded, before flesh beings formed words, a time when there were no barriers between Heaven and Earth. Perhaps clouds and humans were once able to communicate, to affect each other's lives and to live in harmony. It was probably when words were formed and history was written that the growing mind of humans learned how to abuse the gift. That's when the relationship between clouds and people ended.

Cloud life seemed peaceful and serene, except for the storms. Dancing Wind once told her that when a cloud person was storming, it affected the humans living nearby and made them feel introspective and melancholy. Dancing Wind believed that storms, rain and all other acts of nature were not done with serendipity – they were all planned. Sometimes though, Cloud People were affected by the doings of certain humans whose powerful words shot up into the heavens like electricity and interfered with the cycle of life. The chants of a spell or a prayer could have an impact on any natural occurrence to create a catastrophe or a miracle.

Grace once heard that the clouds nearest the Earth occasionally disguised themselves as fog. They were the ones who knew the sights, sounds and motions of Earthly things – the ones closest to human beings and living creatures. Perhaps Ov was one of these clouds.

As Grace lovingly gazed at the cloud she called Ov, she had no idea that far below, Amando and his men struggled to climb Finger's Edge without success.

CHAPTER EIGHT

Matilda looked to the sky and saw the ravenous clouds. Wind tossed her hair in wild circles.

"¡Dios Mio!"

The black clouds swirled in a way she never saw before. *Another curse*, she thought, an evil spell cast down by the angered little witch. She looked to the horizon that stretched out before her like a welcome mat for the impending doom. A thin man rapidly approached.

"Ray!" she yelled out. She saw the tall, frail man holding onto his hat, fighting the gust as he neared. He was nothing like Amando, whom she missed by the day. Amando and Rosa left one morning, packed their things and departed without a good-bye. Matilda found his bungalow empty the afternoon after his futile attempt to climb Finger's Edge. Since then she was forced to depend on her only remaining ranch hand, Ray. But Matilda had no patience for Ray's delicate build and feminine ways.

"Ray! Secure the ranch!" The gust scattered her belting voice all over the land. Ray looked to the sky.

"Twister, Ma'm." Matilda never heard him.

The giant gray funnel was miles away. There was still time to save some things, she insisted.

Ray shook his head and had to fight the stormy bluster to reach Matilda.

"All the other ranch hands are gone!"

"What!" she exclaimed, louder than thunder.

"Gone. Run scared. I'm afraid I'm it, Ma'm."

Matilda rolled her eyes. "Curse that Amando!" she mumbled under her breath.

There was no way Ray could handle the work himself. Matilda went into the house and quickly stepped into a pair of Elmo's rugged ranch boots, put on a pair of pants and went about the chores herself, leaving the slender man to be a twig in the gust.

The fierce wind ruffled her eyebrows as she made her way to the stable. The horses reared and yelled in fright as the wind urged them to flee from their home. They broke out of the stable in a gust-backed fury and galloped past a horrified Matilda, out into the wilderness. Her mouth formed a perfect oval as she watched her only means of transportation disappear in a wake of frenzied dust.

"Come back here, stupid animals! Come back!"

Quickly she turned to her only ranch hand she left on the horizon.

Ray was gone too.

~

Ben couldn't help but stare at the tall red-headed beauty wearing a ruby sequin dress and a feather in her hair. Ben ordered more drinks. She brought more drinks.

Curly Horn was the loudest and most crowded bar in Prescott City. It was jammed with stained tables and cluttered with cowboys.

"What's your name?" Ben asked, ordering his third beer.

"Rosie," she said with a smile that boasted perfect pearly whites. "What's yours?"

"Ben. Ben Zander."

"Hi, Benny."

With a wink, she took his order and bustled to another table. His eyes chased the sparkling, curvaceous body to the bar.

"The Las Placitas Banditos! The Las Placitas Banditos!"

The screaming words shook Ben from his stupor. A grungy small cowboy fell through the swinging doors with the desperate warning

"The Las Placitas Banditos are back! They're gonna be coming to town any day now! Sheriff's looking for volunteers."

Rosie slammed the frothy beer in front of Ben.

"What's he talking about?" He asked.

She looked at the prickly-faced man and rolled her big blue eyes.

"Sam? He's always crying something. Town crier we call him." Rosie took a seat. "Do you mind? I need a break. My feet are killing me."

Ben gestured with pleasure. A smile turned his face pink.

"Banditos, bandits, whatever. Bunch of Mexican thieves no one has been able to catch for oh, maybe twenty somethin' years now. They been stealing from these parts since before you and me was born."

She took a sip from his glass and licked the suds from her vermilion lips.

"Real legacy around here."

"Las Placitas." Ben took a drink too. "My mother's from there."

"So? Mexican kid, huh? Maybe you can help catch them bandits."

"Nah. Don't speak much Spanish. My mother prides herself on her English. Says being American makes her proud."

Rosie raised an eyebrow. "Really?"

Ben drank some more.

"Mexican, huh.With a name like Zander?

"My father was American. Big, blond, blue-eyed German guy from Texas. "

"Oh. Now there's a mixture. Not much of that German blood in you, though."

Ben shrugged his shoulders.

"I don't remember him. He disappeared one day when I was a baby. Nobody knows what happened to him. My mother doesn't say much about him, except that he was either dead or off somewhere having babies with a pretty woman."

"Oh, you poor thing. Well, looks like your mama did a good job anyhow. You turned out to be a real man."

Ben smiled at the complement. He wasn't used to hearing that kind of praise. He smiled with humble eyes and looked at his boots.

"You don't know my mother."

Rosie leaned on the table, cradling her chin in her hand. "So, you're not from around here, are ya?"

"No. Just going to school here."

"No wonder you talk so good."

Ben smiled again and took a gulp.

"So where ya from?"

"North of here. Family owns a ranch near the big canyons."

"I think I know where that is. There's big talk about some wild ranch that has these big ol' vegetables and a crazy ugly woman who sells them. Ya know what ranch I'm talkin' about?"

"No."

Ben took three swallows in a row and felt the beer sizzle down to his stomach.

"You musta heard about it. It's right there, by your neck of the woods, up north from here. There's all kinds a stories about witches and Injuns and things. C'mon Benny. I love stories. Tell me. I wanna hear all about it!"

"Me too."

"I even heard somethin' about a mountain that curves way up in the sky like a big ol' horn. Is that true?"

"I don't know."

Rosie drank the last of his beer and narrowed her eyes. Her skin was like cream – smooth, soft and fresh.

"I'd love to hear about *that* one." Ben pushed the empty glass aside with a smirk.

A short dark man stepped through the swinging doors. Long, gray braids hung from his ten-gallon hat. A couple of cowboys jerked their heads to look at him. Rosie saw him too.

"Well, you're in luck, Benny boy. Here comes Red Charlie."

"Who?"

Ben turned his head to look at the tan man walking quietly to the bar.

"Hey Red! Red Charlie, come here!" Rosie waved him on.

A gleaming smile caused deep canyons in his leather face as he waved at her.

"One of the locals, he's older than God and full a stories." She leaned into his ear and whispered, "Friend of the owner."

Charlie made his way to the table and nodded pleasantly to Rosie, who made the introductions. Ben liked him instantly.

"Charlie, Ben Zander."

Charlie bowed with respect to Ben, beaming a warm smile that flooded Ben with warm memories and familiar comfort.

"Benny here wants to hear your stories. Tell him the one about that big ol'rock. The one that's shaped like a horn." She winked and rose from the chair. "Have a seat. Gotta get back to workin'.""

Ben watched her hurry to the bar. Charlie sat down. Some of the patrons glanced over at his table. Charlie removed his tall hat and placed it on the table between them. Ben stared at Charlie, seeing Dancing Wind in his eyes.

The fat bartender gave Rosie two beers.

"I see Red's found an ear," the bartender said, filling another glass. Rosie looked in their direction.

"Least somebody else wants to hear them crazy tales a his besides me." Rosie put the glasses on a tray.

"That kid ain't from here, that's for sure," said the bartender.

Rosie shook her head, "No, he ain't. But he sure is a pretty one."

Charlie's steep hat hoarded the table. The old Indian's black eyes sparkled with enthusiasm.

"The tall rock north of here. Many call this place Devil's Horn," he said with reflection, " I know it well."

Ben leaned closer. He felt safe with Charlie.

"The white man has many words to describe the mountain in the north. They call it Devil's Horn, Curly Horn, Red peak, Witch's Hat. Where I come from, we call it *álázhoozh* . The white people translate that to mean Finger. Finger's Edge. That big rock is the one thing nobody can take away from us. Folks are afraid of it, which makes it safe for the Great Spirit to live there, undisturbed."

Ben embraced Red Charlie's hat, whose shape resembled Finger's Edge, which made him think of Grace. As she danced through his head he sighed aloud. Ben snapped out of the fantasy and focused on Charlie, listening to him the way he listened to Dancing Wind's fables when he was a boy.

"But, there is a story about one white-faced warrior who dared to seek it." Charlie looked into Ben's eyes, intoxicated with alcohol and interest.

"What about him?" Ben asked.

"They say that when he stepped foot on the sacred land, he offered himself to the Great Spirit as a sacrifice on behalf of his own people. They say, when he did so, he apologized for all the wrongs the white man did to us. The Cloud People saw how noble he was and swallowed him whole, drawing human blood into the heavens. The blood spread through the veins of the universe and it stirred with human feelings."

There was silence. Ben swallowed, as if he digested the story itself.

"Will he ever come back?" Ben asked in a small voice.

Charlie noted the unusual interest in Ben's eyes and it puzzled him. He took a moment to respond.

"When the Great One arrives to unite the four worlds, the Cloud People will return the White Warrior to his family."

"The Great One..." Ben said in a daze, "but the Great One has already come."

Charlie looked at him again, "Who told you that?"

Ben didn't know how to answer without giving himself away.

"I just know. I heard. The Great One arrived almost eighteen years ago and she lives– "

"The Great One has not come yet!" Charlie responded with a trace of anger in his voice. "Who are you to say the Great One has arrived?"

Ben just shook his head. "I can't tell you how I know, but I know. I was there. I found the Great One on top of Finger's Edge when I was just a child."

"You went there?"

"I did," Ben confessed quietly.

Charlie's eyes remained on Ben. He shook his head slowly.

"No... No," he whispered, "this can not be. You are not the white warrior."

"I am his son," Ben confided in a whisper.

Charlie shook his head. "No. I did not get a message in my dreams. I did not see a message in the skies. I would have known. My clan would know if the Great One were here. The wind did not speak yet.

Father Sky and Mother Earth have not yet united. The Great One did not arrive."

Charlie looked deeply into Ben's eyes. Ben looked away and thought about his Navajo friends, of the experiences Dancing Wind spoke of and silently concluded that Red Charlie was out of the loop.

"Beware, boy, all that you see is not what it seems. This Great One you speak of is not the same Great One I speak of. Beware. You are being fooled."

Ben frowned, puzzled. Rosie slammed two beers on the table.

"Took a while. Sorry," she said and looked to Charlie. "You drink that beer slow, ya hear?"

Charlie looked at her dubiously and mumbled, "It is you people who have no control over your body or mind." Charlie took a sip. The suds made a white mustache above his tanned lip. Rosie ignored him and smiled at Ben.

"Benny, still got your ear?" Rosie smiled.

Ben shook his head and drank. "Yeah. You still got yours?"

Rosie raised an eyebrow and walked away. A cowboy at the next table shook his head, flustered and turned to Charlie.

"You know, I am sick and tired of hearing you badgering the white folk. Every time you come in here, you've got something to say. Why don't you go to your tipi where you belong?"

"You got a lot of nerve," Ben instantly retorted before Charlie had a chance to react.

"Shut up, you Mexican. Why don't you go back to your own country?"

Without warning, Ben sprang to his feet and knocked the cowboy to the ground. Charlie jumped from his chair. The cowboy rose quickly and threw a fist at Ben. The two men engaged in combat. Ben's face was flushed with rage as he tossed the man into the crowd. People scattered.

"Boys!" Rosie yelled and ran between them. The men refrained from swapping fists. "Stop before I have to throw you all outta here for good. Once and for all and I'm not kidding!" She looked at Ben with soured eyes. "I took you for being bigger than that."

The men glared at each other, panting and sweating. A hush overwhelmed the saloon for a moment before it resumed its usual liveliness. Charlie's weary eyes observed with quiet reverence.

Ben turned away from the cowboy, wiped his forehead and reached into his pocket. As he pulled silver coins from his pocket, something fell to the floor. In the hustle of activity, Ben never noticed.

He left the coins on the table and motioned to Charlie.

"C'mon, Charlie. Let's get out of here."

Charlie rose from his chair and put his hat on. Ben took one last swig of his beer.

"See ya 'round, Rosie."

Rosie gestured with her head as she carried a tray of beer to the cowboy's table.

"Stay out of trouble, ya hear cutie?"

Ben and Charlie left through swinging doors.

Rosie took the money Ben left on the table and stepped on something on the floor beneath the table. When she picked up the arrowhead, its sharp edge pinched her finger, so she tossed it out the door.

~

Stars pierced holes in the velvet night that engulfed Finger's Edge. Grace felt every beam of starlight touch her as if they were only inches away. The orange moon made a golden glow on the cloud that hovered above her. Grace hummed to the familiar melody that played in her ears as the breeze fingered her hair. She stared at Ov, transfixed by his dazzling glow and warm eyes. A smile broke across his gentle face. His expression changed as she gazed upon his face, in deep concentration.

She blinked her eyes a few times, wondering if what she saw was an illusion, or a spell cast upon her by the mesmerizing night. She watched, bewildered, as Ov seemed to magically produce a ghostly arm that emerged from the folds of vapor around his face. The phantom limb stretched to the Earth, moving gracefully towards her. A giant hand stopped inches from her. Her heart raced as Ov's vaporous finger touched her cheek. She closed her eyes and felt the mist against her skin. It felt cool, yet warm at the same time. She imagined it was flesh. She opened her eyes. The enormous hand was now resting on the ground beside her with his palm open.

"Come," she heard the voice whisper.

She looked at the gentle face looming in the sky, then at the hand. *I'll step right through it*, she thought. Hesitantly, she touched the giant transparent palm and felt warm steam. Her hand did not fall through it, like she thought. A force, like a pillow of air, supported her weight.

"Come with me," it said again.

Cautiously, she stepped into the wide palm and found herself comfortable and well supported by the skin of mist. She was rising into the air. Grace sat down in the palm of air that propelled her off the ground. Her heart pounded as Ov's hand pulled her closer. At this proximity, it was too large to see any details. All she saw was a transparent mist and imagined his face.

The white fog made her skin moist. It was like being embraced by an apparition. She closed her eyes and imagined his face. She could see his blue eyes looking at her. She imagined Ov was a solid body in her arms. She felt his lips, his touch and the strength of his embrace. She kissed the white vapor and hoped he could feel it as she cuddled herself closer to the odd propulsion that held her in his palm. Together, they moved through the sky as the wind combed her hair and a thrill stole her breath. Grace was suspended hundreds of feet above the land and picking up speed. At a distance, she appeared as a flowing ball of light.

Clouds, blushing from the moon's glow, floated past them as they rose higher into the sapphire night. A band of thick rolling mist rustled like a stormy ocean beneath her feet. Sparkling stars shined the way like a thousand flickering candles.

As deep indigo folded into radiant turquoise, Grace saw the land below hungry for a new day. Her shadow swallowed the miniature trees and houses. But something was wrong. One of tiny homes was crushed. Hundreds of cows lay sideways, lifeless. She felt her throat tighten.

"Ov! Closer!"

Although she could not see the face of her loved one through the engulfing vapor, she knew he could hear her. The wind pushed the hair from her face as she saw the items on the ground grow larger.

Her stomach flipped when she recognized the tattered barn, the torn house, and the smashed fence. She realized that there was little left of the place she once called home.

Big M was completely destroyed.

CHAPTER NINE

Amando didn't recognize the bandits when they arrived in Cottonwood, but he was drawn to them. He was sitting alone at the El Paso Saloon when he heard a group of men speaking his native tongue. Amando said nothing, yet listened. He turned his head slightly and sipped his drink slowly.

The three men sat at a worn table, one wore a dirty sombrero. They *looked* like bandits, with their day old beards and sweat-soaked faces, speaking frantically between gulps of beer.

"That ugly woman. I know her from someplace."

Franco had the deepest tan and the largest hat, proudly displayed on his head.

"Franco, take your hat off. People will think you are a bandit!" said Carlos, whose salt and pepper hair was a sharp contrast to his pale skin, due to a drop of Irish blood that mingled with his Mexican heritage. He rolled his eyes at Franco and sighed at his bad manners.

"Heads are made for hats!" Franco retorted with a loud, obnoxious laugh, followed by a belch.

"That woman is a *witch*! Everybody knows you cannot rob from a witch!" Jose wiped the sweat from his chubby face. "They *curse* you!"

"How do you know she is a witch? Because she is ugly?" Carlos took a drink.

"I know her, I tell you, I know her. There is only one woman as ugly as she!" Franco said with conviction and drank some more.

"Si! Si! Franco! The one from Las Placitas!" Jose bounced with the jubilant discovery.

"Impossible. What would *she* be doing in a rich house?"

"But you did not see her, Carlos," insisted Franco, "I tell you, she *is* the ugly one!"

"Whoever she was, she was rich and we are stupid not to take what we could! Foolish men! Why do I even listen?"

"But Carlos, a witch can curse you," Jose whispered.

"Who knows, we could be cursed right now! Then our luck of almost twenty-five years will be finished!" Franco shook his head.

Carlos looked at each of them and slowly nodded his head.

"It is true, I am cursed," he said quietly, then burst. "With stupid men! You are getting old and stupid!"

Amando took his drink and walked towards them. The bandits leered with suspicion when he took an empty seat next to them. Franco pulled a gun and placed it on the table glaring at Amando. Amando eyed the gun and got the message. He looked at the men and lit a cigarette, letting the smoke fall out of his mouth calmly as the men waited for him to speak. It was what Amando did so well. After another puff, Amando was ready to speak.

"I know this woman you speak of," he said, speaking their language. Carlos looked at him. Franco and Jose looked at Carlos.

"She is Matilda Zander, patrón of the ranch Big M."

"Matilda Arroyo!" yelled Franco. "I knew there was only one woman so ugly!"

Carlos' eyes bounced to Franco before they landed on the stranger. "Who are you?"

"Amando Lopez," he said with a puff and a stream of smoke. "I worked for Matilda for many, many years." The smoke found its familiar place on his hat. "I remember the day she came. None of the rancheros could understand why our patrón, Elmo had taken such an ugly bride," he sucked on the cigarette until its tip was red before he released a cloud. "A *nasty* one."

"Who is this Elmo?" Carlos leaned closer, "Was he rich?"

Amando nodded. "Rich of the heart and of the pockets. He was a good patrón. But one day," Amando took anther puff, "he disappeared. And after that, señora became our patrón."

The bandits listened like little boys. Amando swirled the liquor in his glass.

"For some reason, of all the workers, she trusted me more and paid me the best. And one day, I began to see that beneath the ugliness, was a cursed woman, a *sad* woman, born without an angel."

Amando smoldered the cigarette into the wooden table.

"Her curse brought a witch to our ranch."

Jose looked at Franco and nodded eagerly.

"She was beautiful and young. I thought she was a good witch, she did so much for the ranch and for the señora, even though the señora could not see it for herself. And I did all I could to keep the witch happy, so the ranch would thrive and señora would be well."

Amando clenched his teeth. The bandits leaned back in their creaking chairs. Carlos noted his ensuing rage. Amando pounded the table with his fist, causing tides in the beer mugs. The bandits looked at him quietly. He looked at them.

"She killed my son!"

He grumbled his anger, "Should have let her drown..."

Carlos quietly nodded and took one of Amando's cigarettes.

Jose's eyes were saucers. "See? I told you."

"Shut up," blasted Carlos as he lit the cigarette. He looked at Amando. "We know this woman well, Señor. She was a bartender at Casa Grande in Las Placitas twenty..."

"Never mind guns!" Franco interrupted with sudden laughter.

"She could kill you with her eyes."

Jose giggled, "Or her breath!"

"Shut up! I am trying to talk!" Carlos let smoke rise from his lips. "Twenty-four years ago, she spit fire at everyone, but to me, she was nice." Carlos shrugged, "And so, she was the first person we ever robbed."

"That witch made us into thieves!" Jose interjected with wide eyes.

"And famous ones too!" Franco stepped on his friend's words.

"You two, I am tired of you! Shut up!" Carlos frowned at them and the men looked away like hurt puppies.

Carlos cleared his throat and looked at Amando.

"As you can see," he said calmly, "she is the reason we are *successful* bandits today."

"But two weeks ago, we did not even recognize her! She was loco!" Franco shook his hands wildly.

"Oh, and you should see the house. What a mess!" Jose joined in, his face slick in the afternoon light.

Amando lit up another cigarette and shook his head, trying to fight the growing sense of pity he found in his heart for Matilda. When he thought of his son, the feelings of sympathy quickly turned to anger. He hoped she was dead. Grace too.

~

Warped images seized what little sleep Grace found. She dreamed the sky fell like a blanket on Big M, smothering its inhabitants and smashing its structures. The image of Ov appeared, smiling from the heavens then quickly vanished in a sea of clouds that made him invisible. She reached out to the empty sky in a desperate attempt to touch something that wasn't there. She gasped and found the air too thick to breathe. Panic awoke her from the nightmare. She rubbed her eyes and sat up, feeling a terrible loneliness in her heart. She looked at the morning sky and wondered where Ov could be.

Grace climbed down Finger's Edge and for some reason, this trip was difficult. She felt danger and fear as she clung to the mountain's rugged edge and slowly made it down its side, arriving at the foot of it with a great sigh of relief. She sat down to catch her breath and wondered why the trip was so hard. She took a deep breath, got up and started walking.

The closer she got to the ranch, the more her stomach ached. Something horrendous had crushed Big M into shambles. The once attractive house was now weather beaten. All the windows were shattered, the paint was chipped, the roof punctured, the front door was broken and ajar. The wreckage dazed Grace. The only sound that broke the silence was the creaking of the door slamming open and shut, attached to the house by a single rusted hinge.

She walked closer, then stopped. Grace touched the necklace that once belonged to Dancing Wind hoping it would give her strength. She was afraid to enter the house. From where she stood, she saw the shattered remains of Dancing Wind's Hogan.

Quietly she walked around the house and swam through a sea of wild brush. She thought of Dancing Wind and hoped her grave was left undisturbed by the beast that broke the land.

Her feet cut dry branches with a crunch, as she neared the Hogan, then saw the grave. A cool wind sent a chill through her and she was instantly consumed with sadness. One of her tears dropped to the tree stump and became a river in the carved groove of one letter. Dancing Wind's grave was untouched by danger, but this relief brought none to her aching heart.

She felt someone watching her with a gaze that warmed her chilled skin. Grace turned her head and saw an illuminated fog, dense and suspended between two trees. It began to take a familiar shape. The brilliant, transparent presence looked at her. It was Dancing Wind, young and beautiful.

"Din?"

"Be careful," her voice was gentle and smooth, "the power of Heaven and Earth lives inside you. Use it wisely."

The words sent a parade of goose bumps down her legs and up her spine. The image lingered like a cloud in the trees before it dissipated.

Grace's mouth remained open, her eyes refused to blink. *Was this really the spirit of her beloved Din or merely a figment of her tortured soul spilling a warning?*

Suddenly it dawned on her. *Maybe it was all her fault. Was she responsible for the tragedy and Dancing Wind had come to warn her? Was a witch after all.*

A tingle shot through her limbs and sent a steam to her forehead. That was why misfortune struck Big M when she was away. She remembered the anger she felt and the secret bad thoughts she wished on Matilda and the terrible events that followed.

Was that why she saw the cloud and spoke to the wind? Did she not use her strange powers wisely? She fell to her knees and sobbed so violently, the sky cried as well. Rain gushed in sheets. Quickly, she stood up and ran, her feet sinking in the wet earth as she dashed into the house.

She stepped inside. The floor creaked. Drops of water rolled off her body and smacked the dry, dusty floor. Since the house was always off limits to her, Grace found herself gaping at the grand, sculptured ceilings and wallpapered walls. Fine china lay shattered on the terracotta floor. The rich, dark furniture was water-stained from the leak in the ceiling. Fine woven rugs were blotched with puddles and dust was everywhere. A musty odor lingered in the air. Slowly, Grace walked through the house, dwarfed by enormous ceilings and spacious rooms and wondered about Ben. Was he safe in some other city? She wondered about Matilda and felt guilt. She hoped her uncontrollable rage did not kill the poor, tragic woman.

There was a noise. She stopped. Since the squeak of the floor could imitate several sounds, she wanted to be sure it was only the movement of her feet on the floor she heard and not anything else.

Grace held her breath for a minute and stood completely still. She heard the sound again. It was not a squeak, but a groan and it was coming from the back room. Her heart raced. *A wild animal*, she thought, and didn't know whether to move towards it or away. She heard it again and assessed it was human. Grace gingerly followed the sound that led her upstairs and into a room.

A body encased in blankets lay on the biggest bed she ever saw. The covers rose up, then down. Something was alive in the cocoon. She stepped lightly towards the figure and saw the wiry black and white hair sprayed out against the pillow. She recognized the creased forehead protruding from the dirty blankets with a single brow.

It was Matilda.

~

Grace spent four days at Matilda's side, feeding her soup she made from pinecones and medicinal herbs. She burned sage, like Din used to, to purify Matilda's body of its illness. Grace placed cool rags on her forehead and nursed the comatose Matilda slowly out of her plague. On the fifth day, Matilda opened her eyes but couldn't speak. She saw the soothing face and the clear blue eyes leaning over her with great care. For the first time, Matilda noticed how lovely Grace's face truly was, which became a source of comfort for the dying woman. Grace saw Matilda's dark eyes stare back at her with rare humility. *Humiliation breeds humility*, Grace remembered Din once say. Grace smiled warmly at the woman who was once her enemy, not sure what to expect in return. Matilda silently watched Grace and never once uttered a word.

When Grace saw Matilda's health improving, she took on the ranch, cleaned the dead shrub around the house and overturned the soil. Day by day, she accomplished more, slowly rebuilding the barn, and cultivated some sprouts in the vegetable garden.

Every day Grace looked for Ov but did not find him. She searched the sky and her thoughts daily, wondering why he did not come. She listened for the wind to speak, but heard nothing. Sadness followed. Grace felt vulnerable, naked and alone. She knew in her heart that something was wrong.

"Din, please help me," she pleaded with the sky. "Please guide me. I don't know what to do."

She looked to Finger's Edge, a beacon on the horizon and felt comfort. Cloud wisps garnished the blue and sometimes they rained and sometimes they tore apart for the sun to see, but Grace didn't recognize any of them.

"OV!" she cried in a great voice that flew like a bird to the top of Finger's Edge. "OV!"

Her voice bounced off rocks and canyons and buttes and back into her ear. She thought of how happy she was at Finger's Edge while down below, devastation stomped through Big M. She felt responsible. She promised the Great Spirit that she would not return to her home again until she restored peace and life to the ranch she destroyed.

Grace closed her eyes and saw Ov's face vividly. The image quickly faded. That was the last time she saw him. From that moment on, no matter how hard she tried, she could no longer imagine Ov. The memory of his face was extinguished from her thoughts for good and she didn't know why.

Grace searched the sky in vain and desperately tried to remember a song the wind had taught her, but couldn't. When she opened her mouth to sing, nothing came out from her throat. Though she could not recall Ov's face, the feeling of love still burned in her heart, like a fleeting dream whose impression still lingered. *Maybe*, she thought in dismay, *the whole thing really was a dream*, and felt the hole in her chest grow larger.

She felt Ov was an eternity away, buried in a place that even her mind could not retrieve. Grace leaned the hoe against a tree, brushed dirt from her hands and wiped her eye with her wrist.

At the window, Matilda watched silently.

~

That night, the cotton halo that embraced the pearl moon swirled three times before it poured like milk into blackness of night. Dark Horse and his people watched in bewilderment as the creamy fog trickled onto Finger's Edge then vanished in a pale smoke.

The next morning they noticed that all the flowers closed up and the fruits of every tree fell to the ground, unripe. The Indians bent their knees and prayed to the Great Spirit for a sign. Dark Horse closed his eyes and wondered where the one called Grace was.

Silently, they followed the sun until it dropped behind the sacred land of Finger's Edge and chanted prayers.

They feared the omen the Cloud People sent.

~

Grace grew more and more depressed by the day. When the sun rose again, she had no desire to get out of bed. She lay, buried in the pillow that reminded her of the cushioning earth of Finger's Edge and drifted in and out of dreams until morning melted into afternoon. She was so heavy with grief, Grace wondered why her body didn't fall through the bed like a two ton anvil.

Loud footsteps shook her from the dream state, but she refused to move. The feet stomped deliberately closer, vibrating the bed. Still, she refused to move.

"Get up!" roared the angry voice.

Grace drowned in a sea of pillows. She didn't care what Matilda did anymore. There was nothing left inside her to feel anything.

Big hands lifted her limp body from the bed and carried her into to another place. Grace did not open her eyes but willingly allowed Matilda to remove her from the room and prop her in a kitchen chair. An appetizing aroma immediately overwhelmed Grace. She breathed in the familiar scent that forced her eyes open.

In the kitchen, the table was set for royalty. All the proper utensils were arranged elegantly. A sparkling china plate held roasted eggs and a stack of warm, thick tortillas were coddled in a cloth nearby. Hot, brown liquid danced in a gleaming cup. She soaked in the smell, which triggered a roar in her stomach. Coffee sent steamy fingers that opened her eyes wider.

Did she die? What was this heavenly meal? Grace stared in silence, never seeing such a meal placed before her in her entire life.

"Eat!" Matilda's voice charged.

Grace looked at the woman towering over her. Her hair was neatly tied back in a bun, her face wore the usual grimace, but she detected a slight gentleness in her brow, a softening in her pout. She looked at the meal. Was it poisoned? If it were, it would be Grace's pleasure to ingest it for a quick and painless death.

She took the fork and ate a bite. The flavor delighted her tongue, *a fine tasting venom*, she thought as she closed her eyes and waited, savoring the best food she ever tasted.

She was still breathing. Her heart still pulsed. She ripped a piece of the warm tortilla and took a bite, which made her lips stretch across her face. Matilda got up and poured herself coffee and sat down again, directly across Grace. She watched the young woman devour the meal and studied her face.

"What's the matter with you?" she busted out abruptly, causing Grace to choke on the morsel still in her mouth. Was Matilda talking to her? She shook her head slowly and kept her eye on Matilda.

"There *is* something the matter," Matilda said before she gulped the hot liquid in one swallow. She slammed the cup on the table.

"What is it?" A trace of steam billowed from her lips.

"Nothing."

Matilda belched. Grace looked at her, and thought she was back to her normal self. Grace felt Matilda's eyes studying her, extracting her deepest emotion, then nod with understanding.

"Misery will make you bitter."

Grace stopped and stared in disbelief. Matilda looked to the floor.

"And bitterness," she said softly, "is the curse of loneliness." Silence captured the room.

"Don't be like me." Matilda threw her napkin on the table. She sighed, got up and went outside.

Grace watched Matilda without blinking. She cupped her fingers to hide her gaping mouth. At that moment she discovered a new person, one who had intuitive knowledge and wisdom, one who recognized the sorrow in her because it was so familiar to her own. Grace now understood something about Matilda that no one else did and her heart opened up.

From the window, she saw Matilda pick up a hoe and begin to turn the soil. Grace walked to the door. Still in her night gown, she stepped out with bare feet and walked towards Matilda. Without a word, she picked up a rake. Matilda and Grace worked the land, side by side, until the sun fell down.

Grace thought she saw Matilda smile that day.

~

The afternoon rain fell violently. It was as if Ov was crying one hundred million tears. Grace felt sadness and loss.

She stared out the window and thought, maybe this strange love she had for a cloud wasn't supposed to happen. She wondered if it really happened at all. Was this strange fantasy the symptom of a lovesick heart or was she simply crazy? Her mind churned as her eyes studied the sky. Maybe the Great Spirit was angry and punished them both for their secret affair. Did she somehow misuse her powers and now the privilege was gone? She wondered if Ov was out there somewhere, too far away to be seen. Was he a faceless cloud in some forsaken place, doomed never to see her again? Or, was he still there and invisible to her? Maybe they were invisible to each other. Then, it hit her. What if clouds did not live forever like she always thought? Was Ov dead? A tear formed in her eyes. She couldn't think about that. She wouldn't think about that.

Grace was so lost in time, she didn't notice the rain let up. She saw Matilda quietly working the land and went outside. The air was still. She wondered if the wind was holding its breath in silent protest to a love that was lost.

At that very moment, it seemed that everything in Heaven and Earth stopped too. Grace felt the silence fall like a thick blanket as the world stood absolutely still for one solid minute. The clouds ceased to move. The grass refrained from growing. The birds did not fly. The branches of trees didn't dare sway. All of this inactivity went unnoticed by any human being, for none would have any recollection of it, since they too, were still. Every human being stopped living that moment except for Grace.

Grace felt a quivering, sick feeling overcome her as if life was draining from her. She felt as if her skin was being peeled off as a tingle ripped through her body. She fell to her knees then fell on her face. Was all of nature mourning her loss too?

The stillness caused a silence so solid, Grace thought she was deaf. In her weakness, she managed to raise her eyes just enough to see Matilda who stood frozen solid, like a statue sinking fast into the mud. Grace had no voice to call the woman who seemed to have died so suddenly that rigger mortis seized her instantly. She feared Matilda's colossal body would teeter over and fall upon her like a plummeting tree, killing her too.

Grace looked away from one curious sight to see another.

A bird, with its wings spread out, was suspended in mid flight. Nothing in the sky moved. Her heart started to beat faster when she realized what this could mean — a message from Ov. She felt sudden joy amidst the macabre.

The wind breathed again and she heard the sound of Matilda rustling.

"What are you doing on the ground?" Matilda said, completely unaware of what just happened. Matilda's voice was unfamiliar. Even though it was rough and abrupt, she heard a trace of concern in it. Grace lifted her head from the dirt with blades of grass glued to her cheek. She gained full control of her limbs, got up and looked at

Matilda, towering over her.

"I didn't see you fall," Matilda said with furrowed brow.

"You weren't looking," Grace said with a smile.

Matilda smiled back.

Although Grace's heart was still aching, she felt somehow reassured by the odd experience. Something was still out there and tried to communicate with her. *Perhaps*, she thought, *this was Ov's way of letting me know that though he is invisible, he is very much still alive.*

CHAPTER TEN

He found himself naked and hungry, but did not know his name, where he came from or where he was going. The sun was hot and his body ached.

He wandered in the sand beneath a vacant stretch of blue and felt his skin fry under the fiery ball that followed him. A lively cluster of black dots danced before his eyes as he felt his legs give way and his face smacked the sand.

Dark Horse followed a band of curious clouds to the open desert. The wind seemed to push his horse in that direction. He did not know why until he saw the stranger, whose back was red with sun, as he lay flat and motionless, face down on the bed of hot sand.

Dark horse quickly jumped off his Pinto and knelt down beside the naked young man. Dark Horse looked up at Finger's Edge looming before him and wondered where the man came from. Gingerly, he turned the limp stranger over. He was still alive and in great need of water. Dark Horse grabbed the small deer-skin pouch he carried around his waist and poured liquid into the stranger's dry, chapped mouth.

Dark Horse could not tell if the man was Indian or white, his features did not declare a particular race. Dark Horse brushed the mass of long, matted black hair and saw a gentle face as the man wearily opened his eyes.

Dark Horse found himself gaping. His mouth involuntarily parted in disbelief. He only saw eyes like that once before, when he was a child. Blue as the sky.

"Who are you?" he asked in a language the stranger did not understand. The man looked at Dark Horse with baffled eyes and did not answer. Dark Horse helped him to his feet, hoisted him onto his horse and took him to his home.

Charlie needed a ride to Cottonwood. Ben offered. It would be nice to see a familiar town again, he thought. He dropped the old man off, then paid a visit to the El Paso Saloon.

Amando didn't notice the boy break the swinging doors and walk to the bar. He was too wrapped in words with Carlos, sitting at a table, huddled over their sombreros stacked on the table.

Ben leaned against the wooden bar and ordered a beer. He recognized the gritty voice behind him and looked. He saw Amando and bit his lip. The bartender brought a beer and Ben reached into his pocket, keenly aware of the lost arrowhead he always kept there. He put the money on the polished wood bar, took a sip and moved his head slowly towards the men.

Their talking stopped. Amando's black eyes pierced him. Ben turned all the way around.

"What are you doing here?" Amando rumbled in a threatening whisper. Carlos looked at Ben, then at Amando.

"What are *you* doing here?" retorted Ben, as calm as possible.

"Listen, you are not my patrón!" he said with a burst.

The bartender walked to the farthest end of the bar. Ben pulled his hat closer to his eyes and took a deep breath.

"I was just wondering, since you're usually at the ranch."

"At the *ranch!*" Amando stood up from his seat. Carlos watched, with one hand on his gun.

"What, are you stupido? There *is* no more ranch." Amando shook his head and slammed the table.

Ben jumped but stood steadfast, keeping his temper in check. He listened in disbelief. Amando paused and sat down with a sigh.

"What kind of a son are you?" he said quietly and lit a cigarette. "You don't even know your own mother is dead!"

Ben blinked twice. "My mother is dead?"

He looked at the floor and shook his head. "Dead?"

"Yes, she is dead!" He let out a puff, "Now, go. I don't want to see you!"

His eyes squeezed Ben out of the bar. Carlos watched the boy walk out the swinging doors and left a heavy cloud in the room.

Amando took a long drag.

"Stupid boy, he doesn't know Matilda is dead."

Carlos' head swung back to Amando. "Matilda has a son?"

Amando nodded and let links of smoke escape from his mouth. "Poor bastard."

"Where are you going, Amigo?"

"It is time to leave, my friend." Carlos stood up. "There are many who look to hunt us. We must go or we will soon find trouble."

Amando stood up, placing the sombrero where it belonged and thought about Matilda.

~

It took a long time before the plants on Big M grew again. And it was a long time since either of them had been to the town. They needed supplies, horses and money. With the ranch in some sort of working order, Grace and Matilda had enough goods to market again.

It was normally a two or three-hour buggy ride between Big M and Cottonwood, it depended on how fast the horses were. By foot, it would be more than twice as long.

"No," Matilda said flatly. "Too far."

But Grace felt up to it and insisted. Someone had to go and Grace knew it wouldn't be Matilda.

"If I can walk *all the way up* Finger's Edge and *all the way back*, I can certainly walk to the town," Grace boasted.

Matilda smirked at the familiar words.

Grace filled a small cart with vegetables and some other goods. Matilda placed linen towels over them to protect them from the sun's squelching heat. They packed just enough to get money for horses and some badly needed supplies. Grace also packed three canteens of water and a blanket to use as a makeshift shelter from the sun. The stretch between the valley and the town would be hot and dry. Grace tied the handles of the canteen to her waist and pulled the brim of her hat close to her eyes to shelter her face.

Secretly, she hoped the long and lonely walk would provide enough privacy for Ov to show his face. It happened here before, perhaps it would again. She eagerly looked forward to the trip.

All was quiet. The sun burned a hole in the sky and not a cloud dared to show its face in the sweltering blue. She squinted at the vast naked gap of sky and her heart sank a little. Never in her life did she ever feel so alone. Not even her shadow dared to follow her. For the first time, she felt scared and vulnerable to the elements of Heaven and Earth.

~

The small group of Indians who lived in the woods not far from Big M wondered about the stranger Dark Horse brought home. The mysterious man could not speak any language, they discovered, but his eyes spoke a thousand words.

He sat quietly for hours and seemed to ponder the world while gazing at the sky, in search for something lost. Dark horse provided the quiet man with a beaded garment made from deerskin and gave him something to eat. The man with eyes of extraordinary blue silently accepted these gifts and continued to stare peacefully into the distance. He came to be known as Eye Of Sky.

Dark Horse followed Eye Of Sky wherever he went and wondered secretly if he was the Great One they were waiting for. Something about him seemed familiar. Dark Horse remembered the little girl, the one called Grace Of The Clouds, who came from the sacred Finger's Edge. He used to watch her play near the white house owned by the Big Ugly One. Where was she now? Perhaps this stranger knew. Perhaps they were related in some way.

Dark Horse took Eye Of Sky by the hand. Dark Horse led the tall, trusting man through the woods for several miles and stopped. He parted some shrubs and pointed to the ranch. Eye Of Sky looked with curled brows.

Dark Horse watched Eye Of Sky observe the house. Matilda stepped out to hang clothes on a tree branch. Dark Horse saw no reaction other than a mild curiosity and realized Eye Of Sky never saw this place before. Dark Horse guessed that the young girl who once lived there was still gone and now knew his hunch about Eye Of Sky was wrong. He took the puzzled young man back home.

It took her almost six hours to arrive at Cottonwood. She pinched the dress that was stuck to her hot back and took off the hat to finger comb her sweat matted hair. Wearily, she followed the small path that led to the heart of town.

She strolled down the dirt street, reading shop signs and looking in windows. There were new merchants and old ones. She recognized some and stopped at one she knew. Grace couldn't see the woman behind her pointing or the man who stepped out of the saloon when he saw her. She didn't see the small group gathering as she stepped up the wood-plank stairs and looked in the shop window.

"Witch!" shouted Rosa. Her finger trembled and pointed.

She felt eyes burn her back and turned around. Rosa picked up a rock and hurled it at the dark-haired young woman.

Grace didn't realize that a stone caused her to fall, dragging the cart with her. She watched the vegetables bounce in slow motion down the wooden stairs, feeling a hot, burning sensation on her forehead. A merchant with oval eyeglasses stepped out of his store.

"What's going on?"

Another rock sped passed him and smashed his window. He removed his glasses.

"Stop this now!" he yelled and bent down to help Grace.

Grace saw a group of women standing in the blurred distance, pointing. One reached down for another rock.

Grace rose to her feet and saw four men run towards her. She recognized the man with a gun.

"She is a killer!" yelled Amando as he came closer. "She is a witch!"

A curious crowd swarmed, buzzing with excitement.

Grace didn't know where the new strength came from, but she took it and ran. Faster than she ever dreamed her feet would take her, she ran on the path that lead out of the town and into an oven.

Amando and the bandits jumped on horses, welding loaded guns and followed the woman who seemed to fly. Grace heard the roar of frenzied voices speaking in warped and distorted Spanish. Her heart raced wildly as nausea and dizziness fought to defeat her. The sun burned like a flame on her head. *She didn't have a chance*, she thought, as she heard horse's hooves gaining on her. Shots rang out as bullets swished passed her ears. Grace felt the blood ooze down her face and drip into her mouth, salty and sweet. The men were right beside her now, trailing a smoke of dust when Grace felt her knees give way. Before she fell into the sand, her eyes were closed.

Amando and the three men came upon her, galloping eagerly towards the lifeless girl, when a sudden gush took their breaths. A fierce wind rose from the ground, kicking up dust, causing a fog so thick, they could not see.

"¡Dios Mios! The curse!" Jose's voice pierced the opaque gust, like a fine point needle.

The horses reared in confusion, galloping in circles and fled, taking their baffled riders with them into the blinding wind that forced them away from Grace.

~

This was the first time Dark Horse lost sight of his quiet companion.

He looked everywhere for Eye Of Sky, but no one seemed to know where he was. Dark Horse searched the forest and the desert and became so frustrated, he returned to his Hogan.

Something in the sky caught his eye. A strange group of dark clouds hovered in the distance. Dark Horse recognized the odd formation. Without hesitation, he jumped on his Pinto, galloped towards it. He found Eye Of Sky, beneath the whirling gray sky, on his knees in the rain soaked dirt. Dark Horse stepped near him. Eye Of Sky wept, holding his face in his fingers. Dark Horse kneeled next to him and placed a hand on his friend's shoulder. Eye Of Sky was startled. He looked at Dark Horse, then pointed to the sky.

Dark Horse looked up and saw the dancing clouds overhead swirl in a way never saw before. He looked back to his friend.

Eye Of Sky tapped his chest a few times and pointed up. Dark Horse was puzzled. This was the first time the stranger tried to communicate something and he desperately tried to understand.

Eye Of Sky frantically searched the mud for some unknown

object, and plucked a leaf from a nearby plant. He examined it, then raised it Dark Horse's face. Dark Horse watched the silent man rip the leaf slowly in half and toss the pieces on the ground. The fragmented pieces twirled to the wet soil.

Eye of Sky stood frozen for a long time, his eyes locked with his companion's. Dark Horse did not break the stare. The blue eyes dropped to the ground again, in search for the pieces he tossed. Dark Horse observed patiently.

Eye Of Sky first found one piece, then the other. He held the dark green halves in front of Dark Horse's face again. Deliberately, he matched the pieces together again fitting them like puzzle pieces. A small smile appeared, then disappeared.

He took one of the pieces and buried it into the dirt, almost violently, with his thumb. He took the other piece and held it in front of his friend's face again. Sadness swallowed him as he shook the leaf half in his fingers. He squeezed his eyes and one tear fell. He let the leaf go and the wind gladly stole it from his fingers.

Wind ruffled their hair and Dark Horse now understood.

This man *really* was the Great One.

~

Ben stopped the wagon when he saw the body in the open blanket of sand. He jumped off the buggy and took a canteen of water with him. From where he was, the body looked like a black mass in a sea of tan, but as he got closer, he saw it was a woman. He kneeled next to the knotted mass of black hair and gently turned her head.

A sting shot through his body and his heart punched him.

"Grace!"

He put his ear to her heart, then frantically unscrewed the canteen and placed it to her parched lips. She didn't drink nor did she move. He poured the water into her dry mouth and on her bloodied forehead. Hastily, he lifted her up in his arms and gently placed her in the back of his wagon.

Ben snapped the reins and instinctively drove to Big M faster than he ever thought possible. It was the nearest place he knew and he didn't have time to think twice. He was grateful for the change in winds that gave him the extra speed he silently prayed for. Within minutes, he was home again.

The door of the house opened as the rig pulled up. Matilda approached wagon at the sight of her son. A whirl of confusion twisted Ben's brain for a moment. *His mother was still alive!* He heard himself gasp.

Ben pulled the wagon to a halt as Matilda walked briskly towards him, sensing urgency. When she saw him lift the limp body from the wagon, she ran.

"What happened?" she shouted.

Ben stared at her with surprise.

"What happened!" Matilda came again, louder.

"I don't know," he said in a strained voice as he carried Grace into the house.

Ben placed Grace on the bed. Her black hair was glued to her face with blood. Her dress was smoked with dirt.

Tiny raps pelted against the window as Matilda brought a bucket of water to the bedside. The rain outside grew steady, beating rhythmically against the glass. Ben silently watched his mother as she gently wiped Grace's face, mopping away all traces of blood. Matilda did not say a word. Ben remained bewildered as he observed his mother's unusual kindness.

He looked at her closely, studying her face, her movements, watching her eyes.

Ben concluded that this indeed, was not his mother.

CHAPTER ELEVEN

It rained steadily for five days. It wasn't an alarming rain, not a downpour or anything like that. It was steady drizzle, a constant gloom. The sky remained thick with clouds and the air was moist and humid.

For five days, Grace remained asleep, with her head bandaged and her body still. Matilda attended to her tenderly each day, changing the dressing, combing her hair, feeding her tea. Ben too, kept a vigil at her side. Each morning he brought a new flower for her to enjoy and placed it in a vase near her pillow.

Ben did not say much to his mother. He was still too confused and even a bit frightened of her. He didn't know who this new person was and didn't know how to react. Matilda did not speak. She quietly took care of Grace and made meals they silently shared.

"Mother, what happened here?"

Matilda finished chewing and looked at her son. Ben noticed a trace of beauty in her tired face.

"Tornado. Ruined the land," she said plainly and continued eating.

"But, where *is* everybody?"

She took another spoonful and chewed it thoroughly before answering.

"Gone."

Ben took a bite of corn and watched his mother eat. She was a stranger, he thought. She made him nervous.

"I saw Amando the other day."

Matilda stopped chewing and looked at him.

"In Cottonwood. In some bar." Ben felt his mother's eyes on him. "He said you were dead."

Matilda put her spoon down.

"Let Amando think what he wants. Better off that way."

Ben wondered what else had happened between she and Amando. What made his mother change so much? He was afraid to ask too many questions. However, there was one question he was aching to ask, the one thing he was most curious about.

"Mother?" He didn't know quite how to put it, "Grace?"

"What about Grace?" she asked, finishing her meal.

"What *about* Grace?" he repeated. "I don't understand." He paused a moment. "I thought you hated her."

"She saved my life," Matilda said simply and took her plate and fork to the wash basin. She added nothing to the statement as she returned to remove other items from the table.

Ben got up and placed his plate in the basin. He wanted to know so much, all the details, but could not bring himself to ask.

~

Two men came by on horses and stopped near the house. Matilda saw them from the window, took her rifle and went outside.

She looked at the two young cowboys and pointed the barrel at them. One of them smirked and looked at the other.

"What are you boys here for?"

"Well," started one of them, "hear you got a witch livin with ya." He took one last chew of his tobacco before he spit it on the ground. Matilda's nose flared.

"Well, you heard wrong. Now turn around and get out of here."

Matilda raised the rifle to her eye.

The other cowboy tried not to laugh. A day-old sprout of hair darkened his pink face. He put his hand on his gun.

Matilda cocked the trigger.

"C'mon old lady. We're just lookin' for a witch. Hear she murdered someone."

"Like I said, you heard wrong."

She watched them giggle at her.

"Get off my property before I kill you."

Her tone of voice wiped the smiles off their faces.

From the inside the house, Ben heard the commotion and went to the window. He saw his mother with the rifle and the strangers. One reached for his gun. Ben pulled out a gun of his own and before he could shoot it, he heard a loud bang.

The man with the gun held his hand, trembling. Matilda shot the gun clear from it.

The two shook with fear and turned their horses around. Matilda fired another shot, grazing the hat of the tobacco chewing cowboy.

"Stop right there!" she shouted. Both stopped, like little boys obeying their mother.

"You! Tobacco man!" Matilda meant business. The tobacco-chewing cowboy nervously glanced at his friend. "Get back here."

Ben watched, amused. His gun was still drawn, just in case.

When the young cowboy stopped, he heard the sudden pound of hooves. Slowly, he turned to see his friend racing away in a puff of smoke. He swallowed hard and looked at the woman whose eyes were loaded pistols.

"Get off your horse," she spit through clenched teeth.

He obeyed.

"Bend down!" she yelled in a roar that was familiar to Ben, who couldn't help but laugh.

The boy just stood there, confused.

"Bend down!" she yelled, nearly blowing his hat off.

The boy bent down.

"Now, pick up that tobacco."

Nervously, he picked up the mushy brown substance that landed on a pile of horse dung and looked at her. Matilda took a step closer and let the nose of her rifle rest in his hair.

"Now," she said in a maniacal whisper, "put it back in your mouth."

The cowboy looked at her hesitantly. Matilda cocked the rifle .

"NOW!"

With shaking hands, he hastily shoved the slimy substance in his mouth.

"Now, GET OUT OF HERE!"

His horse jumped and started off, sending the cowboy in a mad chase after the fleeing animal. Matilda let out one more blast to further aggravate the situation, and waited until he was clear from sight before she returned inside the house.

Ben proudly smiled at his mother, who didn't return the gesture.

"No witches here, I guess," he uttered under his breath as he closed the door behind her.

But Matilda didn't find any amusement in the incident. She knew the visit only meant trouble for her, Big M and especially for Grace.

~

"She's alive all right. And she's the ugliest thing I ever did see!" said one of the young cowboys.

"I ain't never going back there. I don't care how much money you give me. Not unless I got some army backing me up," said the other cowboy. "And I swear, I'm never going taste another leaf of tobacco as long as I live."

Amando laughed. Matilda hadn't changed. There was still a place for her in his heart. A stream of smoke danced from the sweaty cigarette that dangled between his lips.

"I can tell you many stories of that woman. But don't worry, she cannot win to anyone. She has bad luck." He leaned closer to the young cowboys and removed the cigarette from his mouth.

"She has no guardian angel, so she can only harm herself." The smoke ring emerged from his lips like a noose.

"You're a crazy Mexican, you know that, Mando?" One of the boys let out a laugh. "You Mexicans and your superstitions. Crazy!"

Amando's face turned sour.

"Don't you ever call me crazy again."

He glared at them with dark eyes that meant business. Amando dug in his shirt pocket and took out some dollars. He threw them on the table.

"Now, get out of here. You did your job. Go away."

The two young men looked at each other. They took the money and rushed out the door. Amando bit his cigarette and watched the two leave from the second story window of his small apartment.

He let out one last puff of smoke before he extinguished the cigarette, put his hat on and left too.

"Who are you?" Grace stared at Matilda, almost in fright. "Where am I?" she cried, pulling the sheets closer to her face.

Ben and Matilda looked at each other. Ben put his hand gently on Grace's shoulder.

"I'm Ben," he said softly, "don't you remember me?"

Her eyes were wider than the river. She shook her head slowly.

Matilda touched Grace's bandaged head. Grace shrunk.

"No fever," she said and shook her head.

"Who are *you*?" Matilda asked quietly, leaning closer to the girl. Ben looked at his mother.

Grace looked at the both of them with a puzzled frown and shook her head, pulling the covers even closer.

Matilda forced a smile that raised Ben's eyebrows.

"Rest and then you will remember."

Matilda walked away from the bed. Ben lingered at Grace's side.

"You don't remember who you are?" he whispered at the frightened eyes, then smiled. "Don't worry. You will, Grace. You'll remember everything once you eat a little bit. You rest now, Grace." He winked at her and walked away.

Grace looked around the room and recognized nothing. Her heart pounded. She wanted to get up and run away, but where would she go? She closed her eyes tightly. *Who was she? Who was she?* Nothing came to mind. She took a deep breath and opened her eyes again, and listened to the distant sounds of footsteps and occasional muffled chatter. *Who could she trust? Who were these people?* She felt helpless and weak. She had no choice but to concede to them.

As the weeks went by, her memory showed no signs of improvement. Ben told her about their childhood, about Dancing Wind and the barn and of Finger's Edge. He brought her to Dancing Wind's grave, which left her unmoved. He took her to the cave where they used to play and to the vegetable garden. He showed her the necklace Dancing Wind gave her. Ben desperately tried to help Grace remember, but she did not recall a thing. *Whose memories are these,* she wondered, *for surely, they are not mine.* She didn't even like the name "Grace". She preferred to be called "Gracie" instead.

For once in his life, Ben found he could walk alone with Grace and not be scolded by his mother. In a strange way, Ben found Grace's enigmatic condition refreshing. She became, quite literally, a different person, one who laughed easily at his jokes, one who loved to walk hand in hand with him and one who seemed to love him as much as he loved her. For once, he was truly happy. All was right with his family. Finally, there was peace at Big M.

Or so it seemed.

~

Dark Horse told everyone of the experience in the forest. He told them that Eye Of Sky fell from the heavens and was the Great One they were waiting for, the One who was destined to unite Heaven and Earth and bring love to all things living and dead. Dark Horse told them how Eye Of Sky explained the wholeness of being without a word, but with one simple gesture. They all gathered around Eye Of Sky and wanted to know more. They touched his hand and thanked the Great Spirit for blessing them with his presence.

But Eye Of Sky did not say anything nor acknowledged the new attention bestowed upon him. Instead, he stared off, in a trance, at some far away place in the West. All the Indians saw his statue-like gaze and looked in that direction. They all remained looking, with a frozen stare to the West, waiting for some sort of sign from the red ball that fell behind their sacred Finger's Edge.

Eye Of Sky remained in that position, unblinking, until the sunset lost its color and stars poked holes in the dark. Many of the tribe fell away, captured by sleep, yet he remained a beacon in a sea of slumbering bodies. Dark Horse endured, curious and hoped he would see what the divine eyes saw. While he stared into the darkness, he wondered how this Great One would inspire humanity when he couldn't even speak.

It wasn't long before Dark Horse was kidnapped by sleep. By the time he awoke, the sun had returned and the Great One was gone.

Even though Grace lost her identity, she didn't seem to lose her special knack with the land. The vegetables, though they were not nearly as grotesquely large as they once grew, were healthy and bountiful. The grass sprouted quickly and the few chickens they managed to purchase laid more than their share of eggs. Grace was content. She was in love.

Ben brought her flowers everyday, took long afternoon walks with her and they gazed at stars every night. He never dreamed he would love this new Grace even more than he did the old. He even forgot about school and found a new interest in the ranch.

With Big M back in order, it was time to do business again. Ben loaded up the wagon with a fresh bounty of goods, packed some canteens and was ready. Matilda insisted on taking the ride into town. She had some business of her own she needed to take care of.

Before she left, Matilda turned to Grace, who stood by the wagon with a bright face.

"Grace, you take care, you hear?" Matilda warned, "If you see anybody coming around here, anybody who looks suspicious, you take my gun and you shoot them."

Grace looked at Matilda's serious face. "Don't worry, big lady," she answered with a laugh, "nobody's going to bother me."

"You just do as I say, you hear?" Matilda replied impatiently. "There are crazy people around here."

Matilda turned to Ben and nodded. Ben waved good-bye to Grace and snapped the reins.

"See you later!" he yelled as the wagon darted away, squeaking into the naked horizon.

When Ben and Matilda arrived in the town, they were greeted with stares. No one saw Matilda in years and most folks took her for dead. Ben jumped off the wagon and helped his mother down. Some curious merchants came out of their stores to see the legendary goods the wagon was packed with.

"Ai! So the dead is alive." Matilda recognized the voice. She turned and saw the familiar sombrero in a sea of heads.

"Very much alive," she said flatly and turned back to the merchants gathered around the goods.

As Amando made his way through the small crowd, Matilda sensed him coming closer and turned to her son, "Ben, tend to the customers. I have business to deal with."

Ben looked at his mother and saw what she saw. Ben gave the Amando an unwelcome look.

"Señora, I am glad to see that you are well." He took a puff from his cigarette. The hot day made his dark face shine.

"What do you want?" she said with neither a frown nor a grin.

"Oh," Amando took the sweaty tobacco from his lips and let out the white vapor with a sound, "I believe it is *I* who should hold the grudge."

"What do you want?"

Amando took a deep breath and let out another stream of smoke that trailed its way to his hat.

"Listen, Señora. You will never know what I feel. My wife has not been the same."

He took another puff and exhaled through clenched teeth.

"You don't know what it's like to lose a child!" There was rage in his voice. "May it never happen to you!" A drop of sweat dripped down the side of his face. Matilda watched him calmly.

"I know what it's like to lose someone," she said in a small rage of her own, "and I'm sorry for you."

Amando adjusted his hat.

"Have you seen the witch?" he said in a cooler tone.

Matilda glared at him from beneath the furrowed dark brow.

"I know of no such witch."

"You know of no such witch?" His eyebrows furrowed in a flash of confusion. "The witch!" he blasted at her. "Señora, the witch who robbed you of your luck, the witch who robbed me of my child, the witch who needs to be destroyed! This is the witch I speak of!"

A few heads turned. Even Ben, who tried to divert the crowd's attention with his negotiating, found himself distracted.

Amando tossed the butt of his cigarette on the ground and crushed it under his boot.

"Señora. I want to forgive you. But I cannot forgive anyone unless I get my revenge. The witch must *die!*"

"Amando. I know of no such witch. And if I see you on my

property, I will have to kill you."

"Kill *me*? Señora, have you lost your mind?"

Matilda turned away from him without another word. A trace of curly smoke escaped Amando's mouth as he watched Ben help his mother step onto the wagon. He stared at Ben and wondered if he had anything to do with Juan's death.

Matilda shot one piercing glance at the Mexican who was once a friend. Her eyes enforced a warning.

Amando watched the wagon ride off until they disappeared. He pulled a handkerchief from his pocket and scooped the dirt from Ben's footprint into it then put the handkerchief in his pocket.

~

She felt uneasy. As she stood in the vegetable garden, inspecting the growth, Grace suddenly felt eyes on her. She looked around and saw nothing, but knew she wasn't alone. She wiped her hands clean of soil and cautiously walked into the house.

From the window she saw a man she didn't recognize, an Indian walking towards the house. Grace dashed into the next room, found Matilda's rifle and returned to the window.

The man walked closer. Grace held her breath and aimed.

Eye Of Sky looked around, at the house, at the sky, at the vegetables as he walked towards the house. His keen eyes spotted Grace in the window. Their eyes locked. Eye Of Sky stared at her intensely, then, his face brightened. He ran towards the house.

Grace's hands shook when she saw the Indian run wildly towards her. She cocked the trigger, remembering what Matilda taught her.

Eye Of Sky's smile gleamed from his tanned face as he ran closer, spreading out his arms in a bouncing trot.

Her finger squeezed the trigger. The blast from the escaping lead pushed her to the ground. The rifle jumped out of her hand and slid across the floor. Her heart pounded in her throat. Her teeth trembled.

She felt her stomach twist as she got up from the floor and looked out the window. No one was there.

CHAPTER TWELVE

Grace never told Matilda or Ben about the visitor, nor did she ever see the strange man again. When she thought about the gunshot, she hoped she missed.

Grace sat down in the damp grass with Ben, as they did most nights, to watch the sun drag down the drape of night. They gazed at the orange ball that fell quickly behind the Finger's silhouette.

"I wonder what it's like up there," she said, her eyes were fixed on the setting sun. Ben turned his head and watched the golden light drench her. Her illness still baffled him.

"It's a beautiful place. You've been there many times, Grace."

"Oh, I know. But that wasn't *me*."

Ben smiled as he studied every part of her face. Who was she? Did he know her well enough to marry?

"It *must* be beautiful."

Ben breathed in the twilight.

"No more beautiful than this place."

"I want to go there."

Her eyes held a familiar look that left Ben uneasy.

"Grace, you don't want to go there. It's been nothing but trouble for you."

"But I do. Maybe I'll remember then. Please, take me there."

Ben was quiet for a long time. Indigo captured the orange and melted her face into darkness.

"Grace, you have to make me a promise." He saw her eyes sparkle in the dusk. "You have to promise me you won't go there alone."

"I will if you promise to take me."

Ben tasted the night air for a minute.

"I will," he whispered.

Her eyes cut through the indigo night that concealed them in darkness. Ben reached out and touched her hand. He heard her breathe as she leaned closer to him. Ben was overcome and wrapped his arms around her. His heart leaped from his chest. They kissed.

"Marry me," Ben whispered confidently.

An unexpected gust tore them apart, stealing their breaths as it pinned them to the ground. The wind was horrible and cold. It cut through the warm summer night like a blade, chilling them to the bone with a shiver.

Ben ripped himself from the ground and stumbled to his feet. He found Grace's hand and pulled her into the house.

The wind slammed the door behind them.

~

"The white man is full of hate," Dark Horse said as he leaned over the Great One. "Even you, who are not one of us, suffer because of us."

Eye Of Sky winced as Dark Horse cleaned the wound on his arm. He had never felt pain before and touched the warm thick red that was drying against his skin.

"It is because you are who you are that you are not hurt badly."

The Great One's eyes danced in the sky. He watched a circle of clouds that hovered overhead. Dark Horse looked up, saw the clouds the Great One seemed to be reading, and looked back at his friend.

"What do you see?"

The Great One's eyes recognized a message in the sky and his face changed. Dark Horse watched pain wrinkle Eye Of Sky's gentle face.

"What's wrong?" Dark Horse tapped him, worried about the doom the Great One saw written in the sky.

Eye Of Sky dropped his eyes. Dark Horse watched Eye Of Sky get up and walk toward Finger's Edge.

~

Amando carefully unfolded the laced handkerchief that contained the soil from Ben's footprints and placed it on the table. He then took the Big M carrot he bought off a merchant who bought it off of Matilda and sliced it into small parts with his pocketknife. He lit a cigarette, then placed the diced carrots on top of the small pile of dirt he scooped from Ben's footprint. Amando uncorked a green, stained bottle, poured a drop of vinegar on top of the pile and added a pinch of salt.

He took one long drag from his cigarette, savored it for a minute before he exhaled small circles of smoke. The opaque vapor fell on top of the wet mixture like small crowns that disappeared into the beige cloth. Amando began to recite the words of a spell.

"Eyes to the blind, remove the mind when Ben sees..." he chanted, *"a witch is a witch, a witch for my son, a son for a son..."*

Amando spit three times on the recipe and carefully folded the napkin around its acidic contents. He took the cigarette from his mouth and held it to the linen until the white cloth roasted under the heat.

An earthy smelling smoke rose from the concoction. Amando inhaled the aroma.

"What is cooking?" yelled Rosa from the back room.

Amando quickly blew out the bright spark kindled by the smoke and tossed the pouch out the window.

"Rosa, it is your nose that fools you!" he yelled back as he walked away from the window.

The smoke from the smoldering potion found its way, like the stream that trailed to Amando's hat, to the sky.

~

Matilda wasn't surprised. She knew it was bound to happen since they were little. Ben hoped he would see some sort of reaction from his mother – some sort of happiness – but there was nothing.

"She doesn't remember who she is," said Matilda as she drained soaking beans from a bowl of cool water.

"But Mother, she loves me. She's always loved me!" Ben watched his mother's dark eyes pierce his soul.

"Are you sure?"

Ben frowned. "What? Do you know something I don't know? Or are you still worried she might be a witch?"

"Don't use that tone with me, boy."

"I'm going to marry Grace. I just wanted to let you know."

Ben marched away. Matilda dropped the beans into the hot frying pan, which cried with pain in the scorching oil. She wondered who Grace's real love was and if someday, she would remember him again. Was she in love with a man who lived up at Finger's Edge? Was it an Indian warrior? Or, maybe she secretly fell for one of the ranch hands. She knew the real Grace didn't love her son and she worried about the day he found out. She too, knew how easily love could turn to hate. She knew because she loved someone once too, who never loved her back.

~

Eye Of Sky was tireless. By the time he reached the top of Finger's Edge, it was morning.

The vibrant brush danced in a soothing breeze. The tiny blue flowers that dotted the meadow made him smile. He filled his lungs with the sweet air and stretched his hands to the sky. The naked sun washed his face, leaving his skin tingling with warmth. Eye Of Sky rested on the soft grass and embraced the Earth. The wind caressed his body. He let all thoughts float away in the feeling. He felt light, like the burden of his body was gone and his spirit was warm. He even forgot the sting of his wound.

Small clouds drifted overhead. Eye Of Sky watched them dance for him, swirling into shapes he remembered. He knew this wasn't supposed to happen. He wasn't supposed to remember, but he did. It was a feeling in his soul – a yearning in a place that didn't exist in his body.

A gust of wind rose from nowhere and rustled his hair. He sat up and his blue eyes searched the sky. Blades of grass whipped wildly in circles and dead branches danced in the air. Two peculiar jugs, uncovered by the wind, rolled towards him. The clay urns stopped at his feet and the wind ceased as suddenly as it appeared. Eye Of Sky searched the sky again, confused. What message was this?

He touched the dusty jugs that gathered by his toes and lifted one. It was as light as air. He shook it. It was empty.

He took another jug and did the same. The sound of water splashed inside the jar of clay. Eye Of Sky yanked at the cork, but it was jammed tight. He pulled at it with greater force, his face flushed and the sore on his arm tingled with pain. With all his force, he popped it open. A gas of musty odor soured his nose. He peeked into the dark clay jar and saw nothing.

Overhead, an army of thunderheads began to assemble. A flash of light warned him it was time seek shelter. He tucked the unopened pot under his arm and began to descend as a bolt struck the grass and ignited the place Eye Of Sky sat.

~

This rain didn't feel like any other rain. Grace had the incredible urge to stand in it, to become soaked by it. Matilda didn't say anything when she saw the girl sitting outside, deluged by the downpour.

The lightening didn't frighten her. Nor did its boom. What Grace felt in the drops was something she didn't expect. Overwhelmed with sadness and longing, she began to cry like the rain, her tears indistinguishable from those that fell from Heaven. She had no idea why she felt such sadness.

When Ben saw her, he ran outside, dodging drops and brought her in. Grace wouldn't tell him why she went outside to be in the storm. When he watched her, he wondered about Red Charlie's warning. Maybe things really were not what they seemed to be. But then, when he gazed into her eyes, nothing mattered more than what he felt in his heart.

In her room, he wrapped Grace in a warm blanket as she sat on the bed. Ben brought her a cup of tea and sat next to her.

"Thank you," she said and smiled in a way that reminded him of the old Grace. Ben let the words of his mother enter his mind.

"Grace, do you love me?"

Grace looked at him with raised brows. "Yes."

"Do you still want to marry me tomorrow?"

"Very much."

A smile spread across his face.

"I'm so happy. You don't know how long I've waited for this day." He took her wet body into his arms, overwhelmed with joy,

"We will be so happy together, you and I. Life will be wonderful."

The day's light vanished quickly, but the night that followed, lingered. It was a night that refused to let Grace sleep soundly, a night that interrupted her peace with dreams.

She dreamed of an old woman with coal eyes, who stood on top of Finger's Edge. The land around her was barren and ugly. She didn't recognize it was Dancing Wind.

"Go," said Din, "you do not belong here anymore." Grace immediately felt herself fall off a cliff. As she gasped for air, she plummeted from the sky, landed in her bed and woke up in a cold sweat.

It was followed by another disturbing dream. In this one, Grace dreamed that she and Ben were getting married at the foot of Finger's Edge when a sudden earthquake rumbled the ground and sent the giant butte crumbling to pieces. Boulders tumbled from the sky and fell upon their heads. The Earth opened its hungry jaws and gobbled her up.

Nightmares robbed Grace's sleep, which left her eyes tired and stinging in the morning. She made her way to the breakfast table and swallowed as much coffee as possible. Ben did not notice his weary wife-to-be and chattered away cheerfully, refueled with warm, luscious sleep.

"But before we build the house, we *have* to travel. I want to take Grace everywhere. Maybe we'll honeymoon in Reno..."

Grace watched his mouth move with unmatched speed between her long, savory blinks. Matilda was very quiet as she slid two golden fried eggs onto her plate. As Ben went on about the future, the house and the children they would have, where they would travel, the money he would make and on and on, Matilda sat down, chugging a cup of hot coffee. She looked at Grace.

"What's the matter with you?" Traces of steam from the hot coffee emerged from her mouth.

"I couldn't sleep last night."

Matilda nodded her head. "Do you want to post-postpone the wedding?"

"Ma!" Ben yelled, "*Today* is our wedding day. People are coming. What's the matter with you?"

Matilda got up and poured herself another cup of coffee.

"Why can't you be happy for us?" Ben pleaded as his mother returned to the table and gulped down her second cup.

The sound of carriages interrupted their conversation. Ben looked out the window.

"It's tio Fernando and his wife." Ben went to the door and greeted them.

All the guests arrived by noon. It was a small gathering, just a few relatives, those who still talked to Matilda, Joseph Kilbee and his wife who have since befriended the new Matilda, merchants from town and some of Ben's school friends. Even though Ben always hoped for a grand wedding with hundreds of guests, he settled for a small gathering with his mother's cooking, because he was about to marry the love of his life.

Ben helped Grace into the wagon decorated with flowers. There were flowers everywhere, even in the horse's hair. He couldn't take his eyes off Grace, dressed in a simple white gown he purchased from town. The rush went to his head. He sat beside her and took the reins.

"You look beautiful," he said. She took his breath away.

Grace nodded in gratitude but said nothing. She was too tired.

The ceremony was planned at the base of Finger's Edge. Grace's stomach twisted in nauseous knots of fear. Her dreams plagued her. She saw the guests, seated in chairs outside, stare at her as they approached. Her hands shook. She suddenly felt empty.

Ben took her hand.

"Don't worry, my love, in a few minutes we'll be married."

She gazed at her husband-to-be and tried a smile. She found nothing in his face she wanted this day and her heart sank. What was happening to her? This was the man she loved. What was happening?

The wagon came to a halt in front of the guests. Matilda wore an old dress that stretched at the seam. Her brow was straight, expressing neither anger nor happiness. Grace wanted to run to her for help.

She wanted Matilda to rescue her and pleaded with her eyes. Matilda did not respond, instead looked away.

Ben took her hand and helped her out of the wagon. He beamed.

"I love you," he whispered softly as they approached the preacher.

She took a deep breath and held it for a full minute. The clean air filled her body and relaxed her nerves. Slowly, she let the old air seep out though her lips.

The preacher said something, but she didn't hear him. Her heart pounded too loud for her to hear anything. Directly behind the preacher, stood Dancing Wind. Grace took another breath and blinked, still not recognizing her. A chill pimpled her body. Ben squeezed her hand.

Dancing Wind shook her head slowly with a solemn look that wrinkled her leathered face. Grace shifted her eyes to avoid the apparition.

Perhaps it was the result of too little sleep, she thought and blinked again, but the uninvited guest lingered. The ghost stepped in front of the preacher, shook her head and pointed to the sky. Grace looked up. The preacher was a little confused by Grace's behavior and looked up. Ben smiled politely and looked up too. So did the guests. No one saw Dancing Wind's spirit except for Grace.

The sky was clear except for a few innocent clouds that lounged in the blue. Matilda's eyes grew dark with suspicion.

When Grace looked back at the preacher, the ghost was gone. She released a sigh. Ben's eyes shifted to her as the preacher commenced.

"Do you, Benjamin Zander, take Grace to be your lawful, wedded wife?"

"I do," Ben answered, quicker than the preacher could finish the question.

Then he turned to Grace and so did Ben. When the preacher opened his mouth to speak, he couldn't get the question out because a sudden gust stole his breath. He gasped, unable to breathe.

The crowd watched, bewildered. Matilda sighed and noticed a cloud reaching for the sun.

The preacher began again, but the same thing happened. Again, again, and again. The frustrated guests mumbled, wondering what was wrong with the Preacher. Ben was frustrated the most and grabbed the ring, pushing it hastily on her finger.

"Just say 'I do.'"

Just then, the wind's roar tossed chairs and guests. Chaos ensued and no one paid attention to the ceremony, they were too occupied with keeping their chairs and feet on the ground. Ben, Grace and the preacher became too distracted to continue. The bible flew from the preacher's hands. Matilda's head turned in time to see the bible tumbling down the hill, too far to retrieve. She looked at Grace, then at the sky with wonder as shreds of silver hair were pulled from her bun.

While the guests battled with the unnatural gust, somewhere, miles away, the bluster knocked Eye Of Sky to the ground. The velocity of air ripped the unopened clay jar from his hands and smashed it into a tree.

The pieces of broken clay shattered and flew everywhere. And that's when it happened.

The cry of the wind resounded, filling the air, echoing off the canyons. People everywhere heard it. Even the guests at the wedding heard the enchanting bellow in the midst of confusion. It was an unmistakable voice that could not be ignored.

"GRAAAAAACE!" A voice came from Eye Of Sky's throat and yelled louder than any man on Earth.

Grace heard the voice and was elated. Everyone else heard it too and looked around, baffled.

"OOOOOOOOOOOVVVVVVVVV!" she yelled back. Ben stared at her with eyes that fell out of his head. The guests looked at her. Matilda found humor in the situation and refused to hold back a smile. The wind was now tamer. Silence.

Grace took off the ring and gave it to Ben.

"I can't marry you."

Ben's face distorted in pain. "What? What do you mean?"

"I don't love you."

"What? You told me yesterday...."

"I remember everything now."

It began to rain. Matilda quickly ushered the guests away from the embarrassing scene and into their wagons. She escorted the preacher to his buggy.

"You're my wife. I put the ring on your finger. You're my wife now!"

Grace shook her head. "No, I'm not your wife."

Ben looked at Grace. His nostrils flared. His lips pursed.

"NO!" he yelled. "You can't do this to me!"

"Ben, please!"

He grabbed her shoulders and forced a kiss. She pushed him away.

"Ben, *please!*"

"Don't you understand? I *love* you. And you love *me* too!"

"Ben! I don't love you like that. I'm not *in* love with you!"

A tear fell from her eyes and her voice fell into a whisper. "I'm sorry."

"Sorry? *Sorry?* This is our wedding day! I've waited all my life for this day and you're sorry?"

"I love Ov," she said in a voice so low, it sounded like a sigh.

"What?" The blood drained from his face. He heard what she said.

She shook her head and let the tears flow.

Ben clenched his teeth, punched his hand and tried to contain his rage.

"Red Charlie warned me! He said things are not what they seem!"

"Red who?" Grace looked at him and wiped her eyes.

"I should have known...you two timing witch! No wonder my mother likes you! She found out you have no heart!"

"Stop!"

Ben grabbed her arm.

"Please, let go of me!" she yelled.

Ben pulled her towards him.

"And I bet you really did kill Juan, too!" He clenched his teeth. " I am stupid! I am blind!"

He let her go with a shove. She fell to the ground.

"I should have known better!"

Grace watched him. He was a stranger – a ravenous animal.

"Damn you!" he said and walked away. His rage frightened her. Grace watched him jump into the flowered wagon and recklessly drive to the house. He didn't look back. Grace wiped her eyes and looked at the sky.

She noticed a strange cloud.

CHAPTER THIRTEEN

Night fell like a wall – sudden, solid and black. Stars peacefully guarded the night. The house lights at the ranch were out and all were asleep inside the ranch house.

Grace was curled in a bed of caked mud that glued her white dress to the ground. She refused to return to the house, to sleep under the same roof as Ben. She stayed outside in the cold air and hoped Ov would find her. She was tired but did not sleep. She closed her eyes and tried to keep warm.

There was a sound in the night. Grace remained still and opened her eyes cautiously. A large hand violently covered her mouth and startled her. It happened fast. Rough arms captured her body in a strong hold and tied her in a helpless tangle of coarse rope. She struggled and attempted a scream, but the big hand grabbed her mouth before she could. She tried to bite the angry fingers.

The taste of cloth dried her tongue as a gag replaced the hand and was tightened around her face. She couldn't see the figure that tossed her into the wagon like a stack of hay.

There was a small gas light on the wagon she was tied to. In the dancing flame she saw a man with a large hat jump in the driver's seat. She smelled the perfume of dead flowers.

She knew who this was.

The trot of horse hooves became the only lulling comfort in the night. Her heart pounded and despite the cool night, she began to sweat.

Ov, she thought as she spoke with her mind, *please help me. Please help me*, she pleaded silently, but the sky was empty. No clouds mingled with the crescent moon and gaping stars who were her only witnesses. She stared at the twinkles pulsing in the black canvas and remembered what Dancing Wind once said about them. They were the thousand eyes of her ancestors watching over her. The thought was as soothing as a warm blanket on a cold night. She felt the calm spread through her body like a cup of chamomile tea and sighed, keeping her eyes fastened to the twinkling stars with a silent prayer.

The sky turned from black to lavender before the wagon came to an abrupt stop. She heard feet hit the dirt. Footsteps approached her. She froze in fear.

The silhouetted figure threw her to the ground. Grace could not see the details of Ben's face, but she heard his belt buckle unfasten. She listened as his heavy breath cut the silence like a saw. He stepped closer and grabbed for her in an attempt to steal a husband's right. She sucked a stream of air, flung her legs swiftly and kicked him off her.

He fell over with a grunt that came from somewhere deep in his body. Quickly, she scrambled to her feet. He snatched her arm and she managed to struggle free, drawing on invisible forces. She pushed him with her whole body and knocked him to the floor. Weakly, he got to his feet and glared at her, puffing with short, loud breaths.

"You forgot about me," he slurred. "I was the one who found you!" he yelled. "You're *mine*."

Grace smelled the liquor on his breath. In the dark, she managed to follow his every move with suspicious eyes. Her heart pounded in the crushing silence separating his words.

"I found you!" he yelled, "it was ME!"

He wobbled closer. She stepped back, her eyes locked on him.

"But you know what?" His words trailed into a whisper that died in a pause.

Grace rubbed the cloth gag on her shoulder and tried to free it from her mouth.

"I can lose you too!"

She felt him stare at her in a way she never saw him look before.

"Just the way I found you."

Grace frowned in confusion. This was not the Ben she knew since infancy. This was not the boy who wooed her all her life, who brought her flowers, who cried in front of her. Who *was* he?

He staggered and reached into the wagon for a half empty bottle and took a gulp.

"Champagne," he spit and looked at the bottle. "For our wedding."

He swallowed the rest and threw the bottle on the ground. Grace watched him stumble into the wagon. With a snap of the reins and a holler, he became a silhouette in a trail of smoke.

Grace looked around the vast surroundings and saw nothing familiar except for the violet sky that covered her head.

~

"Grace!" He awoke suddenly with her name on his lips.

Dark Horse's eyes popped open at the sound of the voice. He saw the Great One get up and leave. Dark Horse forced his eyes to stay open and got up too, amazed at the sound that came from the his lips.

Eye Of Sky looked up, listened and watched. Dark Horse observed him quietly summon a few clouds overhead. He spoke again and said the same word again. "Grace!" Dark Horse found a chill in his spine and a smile on his lips. He knew there was a connection.

Eye Of Sky jumped on Dark Horse's pinto and dashed into the twilight before Dark Horse could stop him.

Now he had to find another horse.

Amando overheard the story of what happened at the Zander wedding and knew his spell was working. He knew Ben finally recognized the witch and would relinquish her to him.

He gathered Carlos and the other two bandits. They saddled their horses and headed for Big M.

Amando never noticed the new WANTED sign posted up in front of the sheriff's office. If he saw it, he would have recognized the famous Banditos, in which there was a reward of five hundred dollars. But instead he flew right by it, with his three amigos in a trail of smoke.

~

With the smack of a skillet, Matilda awoke the guests for breakfast, but she knew something was wrong. She walked passed her groggy visitors with wooden spoon in hand and went straight to Ben's room.

Her nostrils expanded when she saw feathers sprayed on the floor and furniture. Mutilated pillows were ripped to shreds at the hands of a violent, angry young man and left in pieces on the tousled bed. A small breeze sucked the curtains out of the open window. Matilda slammed the door shut and rushed downstairs. She walked outside, with wooden spoon still in hand. The guests, who were not many, mumbled and gathered, sensing intrigue. They watched Matilda march towards Finger's Edge with urgent haste.

When Matilda arrived at the foot of Finger's Edge, she saw a perfect mold of the situation. Matilda outlined the form Grace's sleeping body took in the dried mud. She noted a scurry of footprints. Wagon tracks etched the dirt. Matilda followed the tracks for a few feet and traced them to the south. She returned to the house.

The guests watched her load her rifle, fill a canteen and pull her boots on. Still shaken by the whole ordeal of what had happened, no one dared to ask her any questions. Without a word, Matilda left the awkward silence of the house and walked out the door again. The guests curiously scuffled to the window to watch.

"My horse!" Tio Fernando yelled, as he witnessed Matilda unhitch the animal from the wagon and climb up on it. She snapped the reins as her mystified guests watched her gallop away in a cloud of dust.

~

Her lips were splintered and dry. She managed to free herself from the gag that left her mouth cut and dry. She was tired and her stomach called for food.

Grace walked aimlessly, her long shadow followed her along the dried, cracked ground. She looked at the empty blue canvas above and saw nothing. There were buttes and mesas she never saw before. If Finger's Edge was on the horizon, she could see it through the unfamiliar canyons. She recognized nothing in the forsaken place she now found herself in and heard nothing but her own breath. Exactly how far did Ben take her? She couldn't remember how many hours they traveled through the night. All she knew was that she was tired, lost and alone.

The heat scorched her skin a bright red and her feet cooked on the sizzling terrain as Grace dragged herself to the first rock she found. Weakly, she threw her arms against the jagged surface and sawed the toasted twine free from her wrists. The rope left a white design on her skin.

"OV!" she shouted, "save me!"

The sky was empty except for the ball of fire that scorched the blue. The thirsty ground swallowed her words.

She walked on. Her eyes stung and swelled because they were too parched to form tears. She wished she would cry so her tears could quench her thirst. The arid air rushed into her nostrils. She felt herself twirling, spinning, as if she floated in the air. Her head was pounding. She took one more step, then fell to the ground. Weakly, she gazed up from her sandy bed for a last look at the horizon. There, in the wavering distance, she saw a figure. It emerged from the shimmering heat like a sailor from the sea. At first, Grace was convinced it was a ghost who arrived to greet her, but as it approached, she saw it was a man. She tried to rise to her feet, but the ground was a magnet.

The man was handsome and looked familiar. His smile sparkled in the sun. He looked cool and comfortable in his billowing white garment. Grace's heart raced as he walked closer. She recognized him. It was Ov!

She fought to get to her feet, struggling with the force that locked her to the Earth.

"Ov!" she said in a voice just above a whisper.

She heard the cry of winged beasts circling above, in anticipation for their next meal. Grace focused on Ov, whose body glided smoothly closer to her. A smile cracked her dry, burned face with pain. She stretched her hand out to him.

He vanished.

~

Amando knocked on the door of the Zander home. Carlos and his friends had their guns ready, just in case. An old woman he didn't recognize answered. Amando removed his hat and smiled politely.

"Pardon me, Señora, I am looking for the Señora Matilda."

The old woman answered him in Spanish.

"She is off looking for her son who ran away with the bride who I think is a witch."

"In which direction, my sweet Señora?"

The old woman smiled, indulging Amando's rare charm, then turned inside to ask someone. She turned back to Amando and pointed South.

"Ah. Gracias, Señora," Amando said with a slight bow.

The old woman nodded and closed the door. Amando put his hat on and returned to his friends.

"South," he said as he mounted his horse.

Carlos noticed a trail of prints on the muddied ground near the ranch house.

"The ground will lead us to Matilda and the witch." Carlos and the others jumped on their horses. "Follow me," he said as he yanked the reins and rode in the direction of the tracks. Amando and the bandits followed Carlos.

~

Dark Horse could hardly keep up to the Great One's speed. Eye Of Sky managed to keep the pinto at a racing pace. Meanwhile, the only horse Dark Horse found was his cousin's old, fat pony.

For miles he watched his friend kick up a bubble of dust as he followed from a considerable distance. The Great One had a destination in mind, and he was in a hurry.

Eye Of Sky listened to directions in his head and followed the wind's voice.

~

Matilda slowed her gallop when she lost the trail she was following. She sighed heavily and looked into the horizon. The afternoon sun was fading. She knew there was only a few hours of daylight left.

"Ben!" she yelled into the barren yonder, "Ben!"

Her voice fell flat under the yawning sky. Her heart sank and her throat tightened as her eyes filled with tears of frustration.

"Ben!" she yelled once more, knowing her voice was not heard.

~

A cacophony of voices sang a wordless song into Grace's ears and she thought she was dead. A sweet breeze cooled her face and she remembered the song. It was the song of the wind. She felt comforted and knew she wasn't alone anymore. Grace let the soothing breath caress her. The gentle pats of raindrops softly drummed her skin. She opened her mouth and let them quench her thirst.

Grace noticed the small cloud above her and managed a smile.

"OV," she said in a hoarse, dry voice, "thank you."

She stared at the cloud. There was something familiar about it, but it was not Ov. She gazed at the cloud that gently rained on her.

"Din?"

~

Matilda came upon the wagon in a mangled mess, the horse was gone. She saw Ben's body, tossed and lifeless on the hot ground. She jumped off her horse and quickly knelt down beside her son who appeared to be trampled by his own horse. Matilda touched his hair, his face, and his neck and concluded he was dead. Before remorse could set in, Matilda heard shots ring out and quickly went for her rifle. Amando came upon her with Carlos, Franco and Jose. Matilda watched them approach and held her rifle ready. Franco and Jose shot their guns in the air for no apparent reason.

Carlos fired a look at them.

"Stop it!" he yelled, "Stop wasting ammunition, you stupid bandits!"

The men brought their horses to a halt. Franco and Jose gaped at Matilda. Carlos eyed Matilda.

"So, we meet again."

"Why are you here?" asked Matilda, drawn and quiet.

Amando jumped in, "It seems we are looking for the same person."

Matilda turns away from him and strokes her son's head. The men silently watched.

Carlos removed his hat politely.

"Señora."

She glared at him.

"Carlos," she said flatly, "I do not even want to see your face."

Carlos looked away. Jose and Franco looked at Carlos curiously. This was the first time they saw their leader behave so humbly.

"I see the witch killed him, too," uttered Amando in a moment of compassion.

"There are no witches. Only stupid superstitions that drive people to hate each other. Now, my son is dead. Dead by the same superstition that killed your son." Matilda looked back at Ben.

"I am sorry about your son," Carlos said softly.

"He was *your* son."

Amando looked up. Franco and Jose looked at each other. Carlos stared at Matilda.

"My son? Why didn't you ever tell me?" Carlo whispered in a soft voice.

"You were like the rest of them, Carlos. You did not love me. And now I feel nothing for you. My only love is dead," Matilda said quietly.

The sound of galloping hooves broke the moment. Eye Of Sky, traveling at high speed broke through them in a cloud of dust. The pinto dashed passed them all so fast the velocity robbed their hats and whipped their hair in circles. Even Matilda's horse jumped in fear as the rider flew by her.

"Grace!" he yelled.

Franco and Jose immediately started after Eye Of Sky, coughing in the haze left in his wake. Carlos and Amando curiously watched the two thunder into the distance.

"Such stupid men. Why are they following *him?*" Carlos said, adjusting his hat. Amando could only shake his head.

~

Grace heard the gallop. She saw the man in a cloud of dust approaching quickly and wondered if he was real. Grace mustered strength to get to her feet, not knowing whether to run towards him or away. She stood still and waited for him to get closer.

The horse slowed down as it neared her. The man with the bare chest and long dark hair jumped off the pinto and ran towards her with a glowing smile. She recognized his blue eyes and gasped.

She was looking at herself.

She was looking at Ov.

She froze, wondering if this was real.

"Grace!" his voice was soft, gentle and familiar.

"Ov?"

She drank up his face. Her smile beamed and her heart jumped as he ran to her with open arms. The two of them together was a magnificent sight. They were mirror images. They stared, indulging each other and finally kissed. It was a slow, sensual and cherished kiss. They drew strength from each other's lips.

Then, a shot rang out. Ov fell with the sound. The weight of his body crashed to the ground in a cloud of sand. Grace stared in disbelief at the body by her feet.

It was quiet. Time stood still. Grace blinked at the lifeless body whose hair was draped on her ankles. Blood oozed from a hole in his bare back. Not one breath escaped his lips.

"No," she whispered in disbelief. "NO!" she screamed in denial.

Matilda arrived and yanked her horse to a halt. Amando and Carlos stopped their horses next to Matilda. Franco and Jose were already there, watching. Jose aimed his gun again but Matilda hit him with her rifle.

"You shoot her and I'll kill you," she said.

Jose immediately dropped his gun. Amando looked at her with a new reverence.

"Leave her alone," she said in a firm, commanding tone the men instantly obeyed.

Grace blinked her eyes at the still body before her, waiting for Ov to breathe again. She kneeled beside him and gingerly placed his head on her lap. Drops rolled down her cheeks as she gently stroked his long, dark hair, caressing it just as the wind had caressed hers. The silence in her head was deadening as she slowly turned Ov's head towards her. She wanted to see his face again. This was Ov, the one she waited for all her life. Ov managed to become human to be with her only to have humanity take him away from her.

Grace was oblivious to Matilda, Amando, Carlos, Franco and Jose, who watched from a distance. She only saw his Ov's face. His beautiful face was robbed of life. Grace stroked him gently, brushing the clinging hair from the eyes she would never see again. Gently, she bent down and kissed his lips.

Matilda, Amando and the bandits noticed Dark Horse whose tired horse trotted slowly. Franco and Jose were too intimidated to lift their guns again. They all watched Dark Horse, who barely acknowledged them as he rode towards Grace and Ov with alarming concern in his eyes.

At that moment, an explosion was heard far and wide. It startled the horses and made all the men jump. Everyone except for Dark Horse, stood absolutely still as the resounding boom, louder than thunder, echoed off the distant canyons. Dark Horse's horse was deaf, so he was able to continue towards Eye Of Sky.

By the time Dark Horse reached Eye Of Sky and Grace, they were both dead.

~

Finger's Edge exploded in a shower of red rocks that rained from the sky. Boulders and stones shot far and wide pounding the land with craters and new, unusual formations. Remnants of rocks even reached the place where Ben's body was. According to legend, on that day, the sun suspended on the horizon long enough for Elmo to find his way home.

The rugged man with a cowboy hat and Navajo clothes emerged from the ruins and found his way to Ben. Rocks and sand crunched beneath his worn boots as he kneeled next to Ben's crushed body and gently touched his head.

Ben did not stir. The blond, fair-skinned man with a kind face took a deep breath and looked to the sky. The lines in his weathered face marked peaceful wisdom as he closed his eyes and quietly began to chant. The breeze tousled his clothes and grew stronger. Elmo continued to chant, undisturbed.

The wind blew life into Ben's nostrils and the young man took a sudden breath and coughed. He looked at Ben with compassion. "Are you all right, son?"

Ben moved his body and it hurt. He tried to sit up, though he was still disoriented.

"Easy," said Elmo, softly.

Ben managed to move his head enough to look at the stranger.

He looked at the gentle face whose very presence seemed to soothe his aching body and recognized something familiar in the stranger's eyes.

"It's okay, son," said the man with a warm smile, "You're all right now, Benjamin."

Ben stared at the stranger and blinked his eyes. He touched the man's hand. A tear rolled down one cheek. The man gently caressed Ben's hair.

"Father?"

Elmo smiled gently at Ben. "It's all right." He reached in his pocked and removed an arrowhead. "I believe this is yours."

Ben smiled weakly. Elmo placed the cherished arrow in Ben's hands.

There was a song in the air. It started softly then grew louder. It was the song of the wind, beautiful and ethereal, surrounding them. Elmo looked at the thick sky with a smile.

"Finally."

~

Somewhere not far away, Matilda heard the song too. So did the bandits, Amando and Dark Horse. The choir of voices hummed an enchanting melody that swelled until it took over the air. Everyone looked at the sky with baffled yet enchanted wonder.

Then, they saw it.

A thick, illuminated cloud rose from Eye Of Sky's body and formed the perfect image of him. A cloud then rose from Grace's dead body in her perfect likeness.

The ghostly figures emerged from the corpses and embraced each other. Everyone watched in amazement as the vaporous ghosts of Eye Of Sky and Grace melted into each other to create a single, dense cloud that ascended gracefully into the sky.

Matilda, Amando and the bandits watched in awe as this formless, ghostly cloud illuminated the twilight.

That night, people far and wide saw a strange and unusual sight. Hundreds of clouds showed their faces as they emerged from the sky. Some people saw faces they recognized and some they didn't. They were the faces of beloved relatives and guardian spirits that watched over them daily, invisible to the world, until now.

As everyone gaped at the grand sky, the ghostly images subsided into a sky dense with radiant clouds as it began to snow. The delicate, quiet flakes defied all weather and danced not only on the deserts of the Southwest, but everywhere else on Earth too.

It is said that on that day, Matilda's luck changed. Her harsh face was soften by the cool white flakes and she glowed with a beauty that came straight from her heart. That was the day Matilda's curse was finally lifted and Heaven and Earth united. That was the day Matilda's guardian angel returned, as the spirits of Grace and Ov became one. That night, Matilda was overcome the power of love.

~

The place where Finger's Edge once stood is now considered sacred land. They say that sometimes, if you look at the clouds in the magical town of Sedona, you can see the faces of Ov and Grace locked in a kiss. Some have report seeing them in the sky directly above the place where Finger's Edge once stood.

According to legend, if you journey to this sacred spot and profess true love, you too will see Grace of the Clouds.